Every Witch Way but Dragon

Magical Misfits Mysteries - book 12

K.E. O'Connor

K.E. O'Connor Books

EVERY WITCH WAY BUT DRAGON

ISBN: 978-1-915378-65-1

Written by: K.E. O'Connor

Chapter 1

Training wheels

"When we finally get hold of Finn, you have my permission to obliterate him." My wonderful witch, Zandra Crypt, had her head bent over her mobile snow globe as she sat on a tree stump, typing furiously, her dark hair concealing her face.

I nodded then returned my attention to a most important task. I crept along on my belly, my murder mittens barely touching the ground, so I made as little noise as possible.

"Chirrup?"

I swiftly shook my head and continued my expert level stalking example.

"Finn's been gone two days!" Zandra said. "You don't do that when you have an infant to take care of."

I twitched an ear. Stalking a vicious tree rat took a great level of concentration, and when I was teaching someone else this fine art, I could afford no distractions.

I grunted as my protégé head-butted me in the side and blew smoke in my face. I gently hissed at the dragon hatchling I was teaching to become a magnificent hunter. "You must focus. You'll soon have to get your own food. You can't rely on Vorana's freezer contents forever, and Sage has noticed you've been stealing kibble from her bowl. She's not happy with you."

The hatchling stamped her feet, making the ground shake. She was no longer a tiny baby. Hatchlings grew rapidly, and she was four times my size and developing her first set of razor-sharp baby teeth. I'd felt those on my ears a time or two, and they were no laughing matter. This baby would soon be a hard-to-handle toddler.

"Vorana's patience is running out, what with all the smoke-tinged furniture and singed plants in the yard," Zandra said.

"She's getting a break now," I murmured, nudging the hatchling's attention back to the tree rat we'd been stalking, which amazingly still sat in full view, unperturbed by the fact it was soon to be our victim. Squirrels were disgustingly arrogant when they had no reason to be.

"It's unfair on her, though." Zandra stuffed her mobile snow globe into her jeans pocket and whacked her heels against the tree stump. "Finn's been gone too long. And he left without saying a word to anyone, just a scribbled note. Even Cythera doesn't know where he is."

"Finn's off duty, so Cythera has no control over his downtime." I stared pointedly at the tree rat, its irritating fluffy tail twitching behind it. "Stay low and silent if you ever want to be successful in catching this particular prey. It's the worst kind of evil."

The hatchling finally stopped stamping and glared at the squirrel.

"That's it. But focus only on your prey, not on what your witch is complaining about, or—"

"Hey! I'm not complaining, but Finn is out of order. He's been promising he'll do something about the hatchling, yet here we are, looking after her again." Zandra shrugged. "Not that I have a problem with that, but he could have asked. Finn assumed we'd be free."

"What else would we do on our days off? And I don't mind looking after her," I said. "She is adorable."

The hatchling blew smoke in my face again, and I suppressed a cough. Her smoky exuberance could be tricky to handle.

"Sure, she's great, but she's not our responsibility," Zandra said. "We've got two days off, and I hadn't planned on spending them babysitting."

The tree rat made the biggest mistake of its life and turned its back on us. I lunged at the base of the tree and threw myself up it. Within a few seconds, I was flying through the air, intent on wrapping my murder mittens around my prey. Instead, I lost my footing, suddenly tumbling through the air, tailless butt over heels.

Zandra grunted as she caught me in her arms. She arched an eyebrow as she smiled down at me. "Still proving a point with the local wildlife, huh?"

"I will defeat a tree rat for you," I said. "And it's excellent practice for the hatchling. She needs to stand on her own four feet."

"Our dragon baby is doing fine." Zandra set me on the ground. "And the tree rats are fine where they are, too."

The hatchling bounced over and danced around me then ran at the tree and head-butted it.

I looked up into the branches and scowled. The tree rat was long gone, but I was certain I could hear it laughing in the distance. Wretched thing.

Zandra rested her hands on her hips and tipped back her head. "It's nice to be outside and not be stalking something for a change. These woods are so peaceful."

"Speak for yourself," I said. "I live to stalk."

She smirked at me. "You live to sleep on my pillow and sneak a second breakfast when you think I'm not looking."

"I need extra nutrients to keep my fur this glossy." I was so proud of my newly restored fur, thanks to Tinkerbell. I was still stunned that she'd bonded with a higher angel and changed her life for the better, restoring my fur as a thank you and an apology in one.

"This is good, though." Zandra crouched and scratched the hatchling on the head. "The sun is shining, there are no work hassles, we haven't heard Cythera complain about the wedding for a week, and although Finn has left us in the lurch again, you're right, it's fun hanging out with his baby."

The hatchling emitted a throaty rumble, dropped to the ground, and exposed her white scaled belly to be rubbed. She was learning excellent habits from me.

I was considering offering my belly to be rubbed, too, when the faint sound of dashing paws reached my ears. I looked through the trees and spotted Ember Dreamscape running for his life.

"Hide the hatchling! We have trouble." I set off through the trees at a rapid pace, following Ember. What was that deceitful fluffy creature up to this time?

"Hey! Where are you going?" Zandra called after me.

"I won't be long. I have an irritation to deal with." I leapt over a tree stump in pursuit of Ember. Although he was running, he didn't seem scared, but he must have done something wrong and was escaping the scene of his crime.

The more I studied him, the more curious I became. Ember wasn't panicked. His tail was up, and his whiskers were twitching. He was enjoying this run. Was he exercising?

Ember was still under Angel Force's watchful eye due to his misdeeds, which almost resulted in Crimson Cove being destroyed. Perhaps he'd escaped the angels' gaze and was excited at the prospect of freedom.

I couldn't let that happen. The trial to convict Gaian and Lila was almost here, and Ember was a key witness in ensuring they went to prison for a very long time.

I headed to slightly higher ground, matching Ember's pace. He was only young and had all the natural energy that came with being barely out of kittenhood, but I matched him. I sped along, biding my time for the right moment, then leapt and landed on his back.

He squeaked then rolled several times, taking me with him.

I ended up on top of him and pressed my murder mittens against his throat, claws out. "What have you done this time?"

Ember squeaked again and blinked rapidly. "Juno! What are you doing?"

"Stopping you. Are you escaping?"

He struggled beneath me, but I kept him firmly pinned. "No! I'm playing."

"Alone?"

"I'm with Barney. Can't you feel him approaching?"

I shifted my focus and discovered the ground was indeed shaking, and a few seconds later, Barney Hoffman puffed into view, his cheeks bright red. "There you are! And you found a friend."

I stepped off Ember. "You're playing together?"

Barney strode over, breathing deeply, a broad smile on his face. "We're playing chase. I haven't had this much exercise in years, and I forgot how much I enjoy running." He lifted Ember out of the dirt, brushed him down, and settled him on his shoulder as if he'd spent his whole life sitting there. "What brings you out into the forest?"

"Zandra needed some fresh air. I was concerned she looked pasty." I kept the knowledge that the hatchling was with us a secret. The fewer people who knew where she was, the better.

"It's such a nice day," Barney said as he gently petted Ember, who leaned against Barney's head, purring. "It's the perfect day to take a stroll during lunch. And it's quiet at work. I've even caught up on the paperwork, thanks to Ember's efficient help."

"Always glad to help," Ember chirped happily. "It's good to have a purpose."

I narrowed my eyes at the irritatingly chipper cat. I was still suspicious of him, but had to admit, they looked good together and seemed to help each other. Ever since Ember had come into Barney's life, Barney had come alive. He'd stopped obsessing over work so much, and Ember hadn't put a paw wrong since they'd found each other.

Zandra jogged over, not looking happy, and with a fresh burn on her jeans. The hatchling wasn't with her. She must have used a sleep spell on her. We'd had to use strong magic on the baby a few times when we needed to hide her quickly and she refused to be quiet. It was a less-than-ideal situation but better than someone discovering she was in Crimson Cove and alerting the dragons.

"Hi, Barney. Ember. This is who you were chasing?" Zandra looked at me.

"I needed to talk to Ember about something," I said. "It couldn't wait, and I didn't know when I'd next see him."

"And we had a great chat," Ember said brightly, assisting in my tiny white lie.

Barney cleared his throat and rubbed his palms together. "I'm glad I've seen you. I wanted you to be one of the first to know the good news."

"Good news?" Zandra asked. "You're giving me and Juno an extra week of vacation?"

Barney chuckled. "Sadly not. But… we've decided to make our bond official." He pressed his hand against Ember's side. "I've been getting to know Ember for some time, and we fit perfectly together. I had my doubts at first, given he's so young, but he's mature for his age, and our magic blends perfectly."

I wasn't surprised to hear the news, given the amount of time they'd been spending together. Ember had even taken to sitting in the hallowed cardboard box in Barney's office. "So long as you make each other happy and you look after each other. You will look after Barney, won't you, Ember?"

"Of course. I love being around Barney. His energy is mellow and practical."

"Oh dear. You make me sound boring," Barney said.

"No! You're what I need. I've been told more than once I have an excess of energy, and I need to share it. When we met, it felt right to share it with you. We balance each other out." Ember licked Barney's stubbled cheek, causing him to laugh.

Zandra nodded. "It often works that way. Magical opposites attracting. They mix together and create the perfect blend of power. Has Angel Force approved the bonding?"

"We've been in talks with them for some time," Barney said with a sigh. "I feel like I've attended the same meeting a dozen times to discuss our bonding. I understand their caution, though. We know Ember's troubled past, and the angels need to ensure those dark times are behind him. Having experienced some of his magic, I assured them they were. There is nothing but goodness in Ember now."

Ember nodded. "I was led along a twisted path by Gaian and Lila. I'll admit, I went readily enough, but only because I didn't know any better. But I was doing the best I could when I was with them."

"Sadly, that best led to many people finding themselves in trouble," I murmured.

Ember lowered his ears. "I understand that, and I'm truly sorry for the hurt I caused. I'm moving past that now, and it's all thanks to Barney."

"Ember will live with me from now on and not in a pen at animal control," Barney said. "After the trial, I'll be in charge of overseeing Ember's community probation order. I'll ensure he doesn't miss any sessions."

"I won't. I'll do everything I'm told. So long as I can be with you."

Zandra shrugged and smiled. "If it makes you happy, and it doesn't hurt anyone else, it's all good with me. Juno?"

She knew of my tangled, murky history with Ember and that I was uncertain about him remaining in Crimson Cove, but after a few seconds of hesitation, I nodded. "You make each other happy, and that's the most important thing. We need to seek the moments of joy and embrace them."

"We plan on having lots of moments of joy," Ember said.

Barney chuckled. "That we do. Oh, and I've got something else to tell you. Just before I left for my lunch break, Finn showed up at animal control looking for you."

Zandra rolled her eyes. "I've been trying to reach him for ages. I sent him dozens of messages. Where's he hiding?"

"I'm not sure he's been hiding anywhere," Barney said. "He said he's got a surprise he wants you to see. He seemed excited about something."

"His wings were fluttering," Ember said. "And he couldn't stop smiling. It must be an amazing surprise. Lucky angel."

"Is he still at animal control?" Zandra asked.

Barney shook his head. "He said he couldn't stay, but he was going to Angel Force to see Cythera because he needed more time off."

"Time off for what?" I asked. "He's already had time off."

"He said it was something to do with his family."

I cocked my head. "As far as I know, Finn has no family."

"That's all he told me. Ready for more play chase, Ember?" Barney asked.

"Ready and willing. You go first. I'll give you a two-minute head start."

"And I'll need every second." Barney nodded at us. "Enjoy your time off. See you in a couple of days." He broke into a slow jog through the trees, calling out to Ember not to peek.

We said goodbye to Ember and headed back to collect our sleeping hatchling.

"Now Finn's back, he can deal with this baby. No more excuses," Zandra said as she strode through the woods.

"Let's hope he does," I replied. "Although I'm intrigued to know what his surprise is."

Zandra huffed out a laugh. "With Finn, we're always guaranteed a surprise."

Chapter 2

Absent father

We arrived back in the center of Crimson Cove half an hour later, and after leaving the magically disguised snoozing hatchling at the bookstore with Vorana and Sage, we were making our way to Angel Force to see Finn.

I stopped walking. "Hold up. Finn's over there."

Zandra turned and peered through the glass front of the pizza parlor. "Who's he with? I've never seen them before."

I hopped onto Zandra's shoulder so I could get a better look. I didn't recognize them. Finn was sitting with three guys. They wore similar outfits of dark jeans and T-shirts that stretched around impressive biceps. The oldest guy had tattoo sleeves and a dark beard. He was doing most of the talking, waving his arms around and laughing broadly, his companions joining in.

"They must be friends of Finn's." Zandra pursed her lips. "Is it just me, or am I picking up a demon vibe from them?"

"It's not just you." A shiver of unease ran down my spine. "They all have demon energy coming out of them. And it's powerful stuff if we can feel it from way over here."

"It's not just us who feel it," Zandra said. "The tables around them are empty. Even Voss looks worried."

I inspected Voss Black, who stood behind the counter. He was busy with an order but kept glancing at the table full of demons, worry lines etched into his forehead.

"Juno!" My recently reformed snuggle buddy, Sammy, strode over, his new cat form magnificent and his fur gleaming. "Who are you watching?"

I gently touched heads with him, happy to breathe in his familiar scent, which was free from the tang of dark magic. "We were wondering about the new people." I gestured my head toward the pizza parlor.

He glanced over. "Oh! Finn introduced us as they were going inside. The guy with the amazing arm tattoos is his dad."

I took a step back. "Are you sure?"

"That's what he said. The other two are his dad's friends, I think. I didn't catch their names, though."

"Finn spent most of his childhood in foster care," Zandra said. "His biological parents abandoned him because he's half-angel and half-demon. They didn't want him."

"I guess his dad changed his mind," Sammy said. "Or maybe Finn tracked him down. Either way, they seem happy to be reunited."

"And they're all demons?" I asked.

He nodded. "I think so. They seem nice enough, although they were keen to get inside and eat. I understand why. Voss's pizzas are amazing. He's doing a new triple cheese, triple meat combo with free cheesy garlic bread. It sounds incredible."

"Perhaps we should join them." I was intrigued to meet Finn's alleged father. Finn had never hidden how difficult his childhood was after he'd been abandoned, as was often the case with magical muddles when they were placed into the care system. That care wasn't always top quality, and the children were left to fend for themselves or were settled in less-than-ideal homes.

"I'd love to," Sammy said, "but I'm only allowed out for half an hour of unsupervised exercise. I need to get back to animal control or my magical tag will alert Barney. And we're still doing trial prep, so I can't get distracted."

"Of course. Let me know if you need any help," I said. "I could grill you with tough questions and make you sweat."

He chuckled. "Thanks, but we've got things under control. The angels are being helpful. I'll be glad when it's over, though."

"Life will get back to normal for you soon enough," I said.

He gently head-butted me. "Then we can go on a proper date. Just you and me."

I purred softly. "That sounds perfect."

Sammy said goodbye and headed off in the direction of animal control.

"You two good?" Zandra asked.

"Getting there. Taking things slowly." My relationship with Sammy was being rebuilt one small, steady brick at a time. We had no need to rush, and we wanted to get things right.

"Zandra! Juno!" Finn had the pizza parlor door open and was gesturing at us. "Come in. There's someone I'd like you to meet."

As we got closer, excitement radiated off Finn, and he had a smile from ear to ear.

"I've been trying to get hold of you," Zandra said. "You can't just leave without letting anyone know. You have responsibilities."

He grimaced, but the smile returned a second later. "Sorry. I know. I left a note for Vorana. Didn't she see it?"

"All that note said was 'look after my... baby. Be back soon.'" Zandra was being deliberately careful by not talking about the hatchling in public since you never knew who was listening.

"Sorry, sorry. But you'll never believe this! I know I don't. It's a miracle," Finn said.

I glanced at the three men who were stuffing down pizza as Finn talked. "You've reconnected with your biological father?"

Finn's eyes widened. "Who told you?"

"I was just talking to Sammy," I said.

"Oh, sure. I saw him as we were heading in. I can't stop telling everyone that my dad's back. And he came looking for me!" Finn shook his head, wonder in his eyes. "I never thought I'd meet him, but here he is. Come say hello. I've been telling him about everyone in Crimson Cove, so he knows all about you."

"I'll be fascinated to meet him," I said coolly. I tried hard not to prejudge people, but any man who abandoned his child because he wasn't the magical mix he'd hoped for wasn't an individual I wished to spend time with. But I wouldn't dim Finn's light by saying as much, so I held my tongue as Finn led me and Zandra to the table.

"Doyle, these are two of my friends I was telling you about. Zandra and Juno."

The three demons looked at us. The guy with the tattoo sleeves stood and held out his hand for Zandra to shake. "Good to meet you. The way Finn talks about you, I expected you to have a halo, but I see you're all witch."

"We reserve our halos for special occasions," I said.

Doyle dropped Zandra's hand and nodded at me. "Good to know." Up close, I spotted many more tattoos covering Doyle's body. He was tall, broad, and muscular, his tight T-shirt displaying an impressive physique. His hair was much darker than Finn's, and there was a gleam of amusement in his black eyes. "This is Carlito and Bael."

Carlito was the smallest of the group, but still impressively muscular, with a shaved head and a sharp look in his eyes. Bael could have been Doyle's twin, but he had no beard and slightly fewer tattoos.

The two men nodded and murmured greetings, although they were more interested in the pizza left on the table than getting to know us.

"Everyone sit!" Doyle pulled up an extra chair for Zandra, leaving me with the option to perch on her lap, which I was more than happy to do since it was comfy and I could lean against her soft belly.

Finn settled back in the seat he'd left and picked up a piece of pizza but then set it down. "I didn't mean to pull a disappearing act, but when I heard from Doyle that he wanted to meet, I dropped everything. I got volunteers to cover at the sanctuary, and I knew Vorana would look after everything else."

I nodded. Good. At least Finn wasn't sharing all his secrets with this stranger. "We have everything under control, although we were worried. You've never disappeared like this before."

"Blame me for that." Doyle sat back in his seat, his legs splayed, one arm resting on the back of a chair. "When I found out where Finn was, I didn't waste time. And I was in the area, so it was easy for us to catch up."

"Doyle's been looking for me for a long time, but apparently, the care records were lost in a fire. He'd almost given up hope of us ever finding each other." Finn grinned at his dad.

"If there are no records, how did you find Finn?" I asked.

"I heard a rumor about an incredible half-demon kicking up a storm in Angel Force." Doyle nodded at Finn. "I got this feeling in the pit of my stomach that it was my boy."

"Astonishing. To have such a connection after you gave him up all those years ago."

Doyle tugged on the hem of his T-shirt, and when he lifted his gaze to meet mine, there was coldness in his eyes. "You're looking out for your friend, and

I appreciate that. We all need friends like you. And I'll put my hands up and admit I made a mistake by letting Finn go. I was in a bad place at the time and messed things up with his mother. It was the right thing to do for Finn. I couldn't look after him and take care of myself. I was barely functioning. I was dealing with some tough situations that no child should have to go through."

"Do you want the last slice of three-cheese pepperoni?" Bael held the slice out to Zandra, a lecherous smile on his face. "Tastes almost as good as me."

"I'll pass. I've already eaten," Zandra said coolly.

"We could always come here another time, just the two of us."

"You should be careful," I said. "Crypt witches and demons have a tricky relationship."

"Crypt witch!" Bael's eyes narrowed, and he lurched back in his seat. "I know your family. You're the demon eaters."

Zandra half-smiled. "That would be my older sister. She taught me a few tricks for dealing with demons who forget their manners."

"Then we ain't going on a date," Bael said. "I've had friends she's messed with. They came back wrong after tangling with her."

"It's within Tempest's rights to mess with any demon who breaks the rules," I said. "I trust we won't have a problem with you doing that while you're in town?"

"No problem," Doyle said smoothly. "My boy can be friends with whoever he likes, and if you trust this Crypt witch, then so do we. So long as she doesn't go around gobbling down my friends." He chuckled, but the sound was hollow.

"As long as they don't break any rules, we'll have no issues," Zandra said.

Finn's laugh sounded awkward. "Everyone will be on their best behavior. Doyle knows where I work, and everyone knows about the Crypt witches. And of course, you, Juno. We know not to mess with those incredible murder mittens."

I lifted a paw and inspected my claws. "They are magnificent, and I'm happy to use them if trouble comes our way."

Doyle nodded, his lips pursed. "There'll be no trouble from us. I just want to hang out with my boy, make up for lost time, and set things right. My buddies will cause you no harm, either. They were at a loose end and wanted to tag along to meet my progeny. He's done better than I could have hoped. I'm proud of him."

Finn blushed. "I'm glad you found me. Not having family around can make the world feel like a tough place sometimes."

"You have a family!" I said. "We're always here for you."

"Of course! And I love that I found you and Zandra and everyone else. You include me and make me feel welcome, but it's not the same as this." He gestured at Doyle.

"Whenever you feel comfortable, you can call me Dad," Doyle said. "I know it'll be weird at first, but that's what I am to you."

"Yeah, I know. I'll think about it," Finn said. "I've never called anyone that, though."

I rested against Zandra's stomach as the group chatted and ate more pizza. I didn't trust Doyle or his friends, and Doyle's story sounded too convenient to be true. Finn had a lousy childhood because of this guy's neglect. Perhaps Doyle was telling the truth, and he thought he was doing the right thing by giving Finn up, and Finn seemed thrilled they'd reunited. But I was yet to be convinced. And as for Doyle's sharp-eyed friends, I'd be watching them.

The door of the pizza parlor was shoved open, and two astonishingly gorgeous women strutted in. They radiated a primal, lustful energy that had everyone turning and looking at them. Several customers' jaws dropped.

These ladies were polar opposites in appearance. One was a petite blonde dressed in a bodycon dress and sparkling heels, and the other had jet-black hair down to her waist, black eyes rimmed with purple, and the tightest pair of black jeans I'd ever seen. Her heels were flat and her stride oozed confidence.

"There you are!" Doyle grabbed two more seats. "I wondered if you'd forgotten about us."

The blonde giggled as she settled in her chair. "As if we could. We got distracted looking around. This town is so cute. So much yummy energy bobbling around. I never knew Crimson Cove was so full of power."

"This is Foxglove and Obsidian." Finn pointed to the blonde first and then the brunette.

"They're my special friends," Doyle said, a smug look on his face. "I invited them for an adventure."

"And we couldn't turn him down when we heard Doyle was a father," Obsidian said, her voice husky. "I didn't think he had it in him."

"There's plenty more where that came from," Doyle said.

"You've sired more children you abandoned because you couldn't be bothered to raise them?" I asked.

"Juno," Zandra murmured.

"No, she's within her rights to be protective of Finn," Doyle said. "I messed up, and I'll take any beating, verbal or physical, considered necessary to show I'm here for the right reasons."

"No beatings are required." Finn shot me a sharp look. "I'm glad you're here, and I want to get to know you."

Doyle nodded. "Family matters. Blood family. You're my focus from now on. I've made my mark in the world, and I want to share my success with you. With everyone! More pizza for everyone! It's on me." He gestured at Voss and swirled a finger in the air.

We stayed for a few more minutes of small talk, but I wasn't comfortable. Finn looked happy, but this enormous surprise must have overwhelmed him. A man he had no connection with other than blood was back in his life, declaring to everyone who'd listen that they were family.

Finn needed time to process and get a sensible perspective, but from the way Doyle had his group around Finn like a protective bubble of demons, I couldn't see that happening.

"Wanna get out of here?" Zandra whispered to me, obviously sensing my discomfort.

I nodded. I needed time to process, too. There was no way I'd let Finn get hurt or taken advantage of by these strangers, no matter what their honeyed words revealed.

"We'll get out of your way." Zandra stood and lifted me onto her shoulder. "You must have a lot of catching up to do."

"You can stay," Finn said. "You don't mind, do you, Doyle?"

"Stay if you like. After this, we were gonna walk around town and see some of Finn's favorite haunts," Doyle said.

"I've seen Crimson Cove plenty of times." Zandra looked hard at Finn. "We'll catch up soon."

Finn nodded, but his attention was back on his father, who had a hand firmly on his shoulder.

We said our goodbyes and headed out of the pizza parlor.

Zandra walked along quietly for a moment. "That was unexpected."

"It left a sulfurous taste in my mouth." I looked back at the pizza parlor. "We need to watch Finn and his new family. They smell like trouble to me."

Chapter 3
Wedding wonders

"Did this guy claiming to be Finn's dad look anything like him?" Sorcha Creer was seated at the table in Vorana's kitchen. We'd just finished updating Sorcha, Vorana, and Sage about meeting Finn's father and his friends at the pizza parlor yesterday.

"Not particularly." Zandra sipped from her coffee. "Finn must take after his mother."

"Or Doyle's a fake," I murmured. "I'm unable to get my head around why he suddenly looked Finn up after all these years. There must be something in it for him."

"Maybe he's grown a conscience." Vorana separated Sage and the hatchling, who were tussling in one corner, then she sat the hatchling on the mat by the back door. "Two minutes on the naughty mat for you. You're not to play with Sage anymore. You're too rough with her."

"I'll best that irritating critter any day." Sage was on her side, her harness tipped over as she waggled her front paws.

"I'm sure you can, but let's not put that to the test anymore." Vorana righted Sage then gently lifted her into a seat at the table so she could enjoy her mackerel breakfast. "You said Finn seemed happy. He has no suspicions about this guy not being legit?"

I shook my head as I waited for my own mackerel to arrive on my plate, filleted and warm. "I don't think I've ever seen Finn so happy. He was acting star-struck."

"He doesn't often talk about his past, but the things that slip out reveal it was miserable," Sorcha said. "He was badly treated by the care system, and the foster families who took him in didn't do an amazing job. Maybe he's always held a secret desire to meet his actual family."

"Blood does not make a family," I said. "There are perfect examples of blended families all around us that have nothing to do with genetic similarities."

Zandra reached over and scratched between my ears. "And we get that, but angels are old school. Beginning of time old school. When you have such ancient traditions and values, they're hard to change. Finn is still a half-angel."

"And as we've seen from Cythera and Maverick's upcoming wedding, those traditions are tricky to budge, and problems rear up when angels behave out of character." Vorana delivered my mackerel then slid into a seat to enjoy her own breakfast.

I decided not to grumble anymore and enjoy my food, but I was suspicious of this new arrival in Crimson Cove. Why show up now? Did Finn have something Doyle wanted? He earned a decent salary from working at Angel Force, but it wasn't eye-watering, and he had his own home, but it was nothing palatial.

"We should be happy for Finn," Sorcha said. "He's had a tricky time lately." She glanced at the grumpy hatchling, who had her back to us while she waited for her time out to end so she could join us for breakfast.

"We are happy," I said, "but also cautious. There are few demons in this world who have a pure heart."

"Let's give Doyle the benefit of the doubt until he puts a foot wrong," Vorana said.

"And risk Finn?" I shook my head. "I'll be watching. And I'll step in at the first sign of trouble."

"You made it clear to Doyle and his friends you thought little of them when we met," Zandra said. "He'll pause before trying anything shady, knowing he's under such steely scrutiny."

I hoovered up a lump of mackerel and smacked my lips together. "Some demons tend to act rather than think. They're dangerously impulsive."

The front door slammed open, and Cythera flew into the kitchen, landing in a swirl of warm air and fluttering white feathers.

We froze in our seats, and my gaze darted to the misbehaving dragon on the naughty mat.

"Cythera!" Vorana jumped from her seat and attempted to shield the hatchling with her body. "Was I expecting you for breakfast?"

"I need help to choose confetti types. Did you know there were different types? What's the point of that?" Cythera pulled two large bags off her back. "Maverick has put me in charge of the confetti, and I know nothing about it. He told me to test it! How am I supposed to do that?" She glared at the bags of tiny colored shapes as if they'd just said something rude about her wings.

"Well, it's typical with confetti to have guests throw it over the happy couple." I slid from my seat and walked toward the hallway, hoping Cythera would turn and not spot the hatchling.

Cythera's angry glare followed me. "I know that! I'm not an imbecile. What do I care about confetti? I won't be throwing it." She jiggled the bags. "I don't even want the messy stuff at the wedding, but Maverick thinks it'll be fun."

The hatchling gave a most unladylike burp.

"Pardon me," Sage said. "It's the mackerel. It's the fishy gift that keeps on giving for hours after you've eaten."

Cythera eyed Sage with distaste. "Maverick will know if I haven't tested it properly. I need your advice. Which one is best?"

"We're hardly wedding experts," Sorcha said. "None of us have ever married."

"You've been to weddings, though. You must have thrown confetti. Test what's in these bags." Cythera slung a bag at Sorcha. "Pick one for me."

"We'll help you," Vorana said. "Why not take a seat in the living room, and I'll bring through coffee?"

"Here is fine." Cythera looked around for a chair, and her gaze finally settled on the hatchling. "What in the name of all things heavenly is that?"

"Oh! You've not met my recent foster?" Vorana shot a worried look in my direction. "This is... um... the as yet unnamed baby."

"Why have you got a dragon hatchling in your kitchen?" Cythera strode over to her, her wings flared.

The baby turned and growled at Cythera, her own wings splaying.

I dashed over and stood in front of the hatchling before she let rip with her newly acquired flame and burned Cythera to a crisp. "Don't scare her! She's only a baby. If you keep glowering at her like that, you'll regret it."

"She may be young, but she breathes fire. She shouldn't be here," Cythera said. "Vorana, why are you fostering a dragon? Why aren't the dragons looking after their own infant?"

"It's a long, boring, and dctailcd story you won't be interested in," I said. "And we have wedding confetti to test. That's your priority. Shall we?"

"I should have been informed," Cythera said.

"Dragons are animals, so they fall under our jurisdiction." Zandra joined me, adding another body barrier between the hatchling and Cythera. "We know all about her at animal control. We needed a space for the hatchling, and Vorana was happy to offer her backyard. It's got a secure, fireproof shed, so it was an easy match."

"You haven't answered my question as to why the dragons needed someone to look after their infant,"

Cythera said. "Surely, they're better equipped to care for one of their own. And why come here? There are no dragon colonies in Crimson Cove."

"So many questions, when you should focus on your wedding," I said.

"I'm asking questions because I don't want a dragon burning down my wedding. It's a week away."

Vorana caught hold of Cythera's shoulders and looked up into her face. "Everything's under control. Dragons won't fly in and pillage your wedding and ruin things. We've got a handle on this. You need to relax and take deep breaths. Juno is right. The only thing you need to focus on is your wedding." She guided Cythera to a seat and eased her into it.

Cythera's gaze remained suspicious as it settled on the hatchling. "She does seem well-behaved. I've heard hatchlings can be frustratingly boisterous."

"She never misbehaves," I said. "This is the perfect baby."

Sage grunted but said nothing to contradict me. We cautiously returned to our seats, although Vorana remained by the hatchling since Cythera was now sitting in her chair.

"How's everything going with the wedding?" Sorcha asked.

Cythera tore her gaze from the hatchling. "Surprisingly good. My mother-in-law has backed off as she promised she would, and Maverick is being annoyingly sweet, although he barely leaves me alone. And he has so many questions about the wedding. I dream of weddings, these days. Every dream is full of white things, flowers, and cake."

"That's good! You're focused," I said. "And Maverick asks questions because he wants the wedding to be perfect. That's a sign of good character. He's taking care of you to make sure your special day is one you remember."

"So long as I don't remember the day because a small fire-breathing creature roams through it, causing havoc."

"The hatchling won't be at your wedding," Vorana said. "She has a comfortable, secure pen she goes into when she needs quiet time. I can check on her using a monitor. Forget about the hatchling."

"She's impossible to forget. She's brilliant white and standing on your kitchen mat." Cythera shook her head and huffed out a breath. "I should have been told she was here."

"What about your wedding cake?" I asked hurriedly, eager to get her focus away from the baby. "Any progress in finding a replacement baker?"

Cythera nodded. "After a lengthy conversation with the higher angels, they've agreed Tia will make my cake."

"Tia's cakes are delicious," Vorana said. "She won't let you down."

A brief smile flickered across Cythera's face. "I'm glad she's doing it. I'm not one for fancy cakes, and although Gertrude baked amazing treats, angel rest her soul, they were too rich for me. I've asked Tia to keep things simple. I want a layer of plain vanilla. That's my favorite."

"Whatever you want for your perfect day," Vorana said. "We're all looking forward to it."

Cythera waved away an offer of coffee. "I'm almost looking forward to it too. I suspect you all know I've had doubts, but Maverick has remained true. With me almost being poisoned, and the shock of learning Maverick's best man was trying to break us up, it could have destroyed us, but those tests brought us closer together."

"Don't sound so surprised," I said. "You're an excellent angel, and Maverick is a solid, decent guy, so you're perfect together. And he adores you. Perhaps you could open your heart to him over time."

Cythera arched a pale brow, and I expected her to tell me to mind my own business. "It's something I'm considering. Right now, I must decide about the ridiculous confetti. Star-shaped or round? Which is best?"

I gestured for Sorcha to open the bags. "We can test it with the hatchling. She loves to play." I motioned at the baby to join us since she'd served her time out on the kitchen mat then delved into the first bag of confetti and pulled out pawfuls of star-shaped multi-colored paper. I tossed it into the air, and the hatchling bounced around as it fell, huffing out smoke to lift the star shapes higher.

We repeated the exercise several times and then turned our attention to the round confetti. Even Sage joined in, leaping off her chair and batting stray pieces of confetti with her paws.

"When is Finn back at work?" Zandra asked Cythera.

"Not until next week. He wanted more time off, and I'm fine with him having a few extra days. It's been quiet in Crimson Cove. We've had no murders for almost a month." She nudged me with her foot. "And I'd like it to stay that way."

"As do we. But if you ever need expert backup, you know where we are." I tossed a pawful of star confetti at the hatchling, and she snapped at it with her teeth.

"Look at the state of my kitchen." Vorana was smiling as she shook her head. "I'll be finding confetti in crevices for weeks after this."

"We have to test it thoroughly," I said. "And it looks like the hatchling prefers the star confetti."

The baby was covered in stars as she swirled around and chirped her enjoyment.

Cythera pursed her lips. "You'd better not be hiding anything from me about her. I don't think I've ever heard of dragons abandoning one of their own. Babies are much cherished in their community."

"The hatchling is in good hands and paws," I assured her. "You have nothing to worry about."

"I have a thousand things to worry about, and I don't need that added to the list." She pointed at the hatchling, who snarled at Cythera and then spun, sending stars swirling around the kitchen.

"This wonderful creature just solved your confetti dilemma," I said. "The star shapes float better and look prettier. You can tell Maverick you've extensively tested it and that's your choice."

Cythera grabbed the half-empty bags of confetti. "It's something. But if I get any reports of a rampaging hatchling—"

"She won't rampage. Now, go tell Maverick the excellent news about the confetti," I said.

Cythera glared at the hatchling for another second then nodded and swept out of the kitchen.

We all looked at each other and slumped into our seats. The hatchling bounced over and grabbed my paw in her mouth, almost dragging me to the floor.

"You'll be back on the naughty mat if you don't behave," I warned her, tugging my paw out of her mouth.

"I'm in shock," Vorana said. "Cythera almost smiled. She seems... dare I say it, happy!"

"She was half as snappy as usual," Sorcha said. "And she talked to us rather than barking out single-word commands and expecting us to obey."

"This wedding is a good thing," Zandra said. "If Cythera had seen the hatchling under any other circumstances, she'd never have let it go."

"Distractions are what we need," I said. "If Cythera thinks too much about how odd it is that Vorana has a baby dragon living with her, she'll probe, and that's when things go wrong."

"This wedding will be the making of Cythera." Vorana grinned. "I can't wait to see how she looks in her gown."

"She'll be dazzling, so long as she smiles," I said.

"I... err... I have something to tell you about the wedding," Sorcha said.

"You're still going, aren't you?" Vorana asked.

Sorcha ducked her head. "Yes. But... I have a date coming with me. It's one of Remus's new vampires. He only moved into the hive house a month ago, but he's been coming to the café most days. He's cute. And he seems sweet. Nothing like Gaian."

I gave a huge, catlike smile as Sorcha talked more about her date. She'd been cautious about getting back into the romance game ever since her heart got broken by the deceitful Gaian, but she was finally healing, and I was glad to see her happy again.

"Everything is working out," I said. "Vorana will go to the wedding with Sage. I'll take Sammy. Sorcha has her new vampire boyfriend to entertain her, and Zandra will go with Randal."

"Hey! He hasn't even asked me to be his wedding date," Zandra said. "And I figured we'd go together. You don't mind me third-wheeling it with you and Sammy, do you?"

"Randal will ask you. He just takes his time with important things." I sat back as a sense of contentment filled me. Everything felt perfect.

I'd just finished my breakfast when Zandra's mobile snow globe buzzed, and she pulled it out to check the message. Her eyes widened, and her face paled. She shoved her seat back and stood.

"Is something wrong?" Vorana asked.

"No! Just got something to do." She grabbed me and settled me on her shoulder. "See you later."

"What's so urgent we have to do it now?" I asked after Zandra had shut the front door behind her and leaned against it.

"This!" She showed me the message that had arrived on her globe. It was from Finn.
Help. I've murdered my dad.

Chapter 4

Here comes trouble

"Is this his idea of a joke?" I'd read Finn's message several times and still couldn't believe it.

"If it is, I'm not laughing." Zandra scowled at her mobile snow globe. "The message doesn't say where he is."

"I'll find our mysterious angel friend." I flicked out a paw, casting a spell to locate Finn. A wispy map of Crimson Cove appeared in the air, and a light orb floated around it several times before settling on a street.

Zandra cast a translocation spell, and we arrived on Mistley Avenue. "What number?"

I recast the location spell. Now we were in the right area, it would be simple for magic to identify Finn. Location spells worked better when you had an item belonging to the person or a drop of their blood, but I knew Finn so well that I could find him without additional help.

"Number seventy-two." I gestured to the right-hand side of the street.

Zandra jogged along with me on her shoulder. Her silence spoke volumes. She was worried. Finn joked around sometimes, but never anything like this. And I had a terrible feeling in my gut that something was wrong.

We reached the house, a large single-story detached property with a neat front yard and white painted walls. Zandra dashed to the front door and knocked then tried the handle. It was locked. She knocked again. "Finn! It's Zandra and Juno. Are you inside?"

There was no reply.

"Try the windows," I said. "We may be able to see something or find one open."

Zandra headed to the window closest to the front door and peered inside. She gasped. There was a body on the floor.

"That's Doyle," I said. "I recognize the tattoo sleeve. Where is Finn?"

Zandra tried the window, but it was locked, so we dashed around the outside of the house. She tried the door handle on the back entrance, and it opened a few inches before meeting resistance.

I peered through the glass. Finn was on the floor! "Hurry, get inside. Finn's in trouble."

Zandra shoved her shoulder against the door and heaved, creating a gap large enough for us to squeeze through. The second we entered the kitchen, the stench of burning, sulfur, and blood almost overwhelmed me.

I hopped off Zandra's shoulder as she crouched beside Finn. He was passed out, slumped to one side. There was blood on the side of his head, and his wings and hands were badly burned.

"Finn! It's Zandra. Can you hear me?" Zandra checked his pulse and nodded at me. "He's still alive."

Finn groaned, and his eyelids flickered.

"Take your time. It looks like you've had a knock on the head," I said. "And be careful with your hands. You've got nasty burns."

"My dad," he murmured.

"Juno, go see how Doyle's doing," Zandra said. "I'll stay with Finn."

I dashed to the front room and discovered Doyle. Fire had destroyed his wings, and the stench of sulfur and demon was everywhere. I hopped quickly over the charred remains of the rug Doyle had fallen on and checked for signs of life, but it was easy to see from the devastation on his body that he was long gone.

I looked around the room. Fire damage marred every surface. Whatever magic had been used to attack Doyle and Finn was powerful. It would need to be to overwhelm two strong magical beings.

There was a yelp from the kitchen. I dashed back to see Finn grappling with Zandra. He had one hand around her throat and was thumping her with his free hand.

I raced over and launched myself at his chest, whacking into him and knocking him back to the floor. I pinned him with my murder mittens and hissed in his face. "Calm yourself. We're here to help. It's Juno and Zandra. Focus! We're friends."

Finn's head slumped back, and he lost consciousness again, but he was alert a few seconds later. "Sorry. My head is a mess. I don't know what's going on."

"Stay where you are," Zandra said, rubbing her arm as she kneeled beside him. "Something bad went down here, and you were in the middle of it. You could have a concussion. You've got a massive lump on the side of your head."

"Tell us what happened," I said.

Finn heaved out a sigh and then winced as if taking a breath hurt him. "Is he dead?"

"I've been to check. There was nothing I could do to save Doyle," I said. "I'm sorry."

No one spoke for several minutes as this unwelcome news filtered through us and settled in as our new grim reality.

"Finn, you sent me a message saying you think you killed Doyle," Zandra said. "Why did you do that?"

He kept his eyes shut. "Look at the state of me! I woke up next to him like this."

"You're bloody, bruised, and burned, but that doesn't mean you killed him," I said.

Finn lifted one hand. "There's evidence of demon flame in that room. It was only the two of us in the house last night. We stayed up late talking and drinking."

"And then what?" Zandra asked. "Did you argue?"

"We had some heated debates. Doyle wasn't keen on talking about why he abandoned me. I was annoyed. I... I said a few things."

"Did you confront him and a fight erupted?" I settled more comfortably on Finn's chest now he was no longer trying to obliterate Zandra.

Finn went quiet again. "I don't remember."

"What do you remember?"

"I remember us sitting in the front room, and I was feeling tired but not wanting to go to sleep because I didn't want the day to end."

"What happened next?"

"This! I came to, and there was a fire burning in the room. I panicked and put it out. There was so much mess and chaos, and when I saw Doyle on the floor, it took me a few seconds to process it. I tried to help him, but demon flame had burned him."

"You were alone all night?" I asked. "What about your dad's friends?"

"They were here for a short while, but they didn't stay. They headed off soon after we'd eaten at the pizza parlor."

"Why this house?" Zandra asked. "What were you doing here?"

"Doyle is renting it. He's staying in Crimson Cove for a couple of weeks while we get to know each other." Finn eased himself up onto his elbows. "It was just the two of us. And I remember Doyle locking the doors. No one could have gotten in."

"The back door was unlocked when we arrived," Zandra said.

"Because I unlocked it before passing out. I woke up, put out the flames, then checked on my dad. I must have sent you the message after that, but I don't remember doing it. My memory is so hazy."

"If you have gaps in your memory," I said, "it's possible you don't remember someone breaking in and attacking you and Doyle."

Finn blew out a breath. "Why would anyone do that, though?"

"Why would *you* attack Doyle?" Zandra asked.

"I don't remember doing it! But only insanely strong fire magic would have done that to him. And look at me. I could have used my demon flame and injured myself." He lifted his damaged hands. "Maybe I attacked Doyle, and he fought back. That's how I got burned, too." There were tears in Finn's eyes, along with a swirl of confusion and pain. "What did I do?"

"Rest for now and heal," I said. "We trust you. You'd never do this. And you were excited to introduce us to Doyle. You were happy he was here."

"I was." Finn went quiet for a stretch of time. "And although I wouldn't want to hurt him, you've met my demon side. When he takes over, I'm not always in control. What if being around Doyle and his demon friends triggered something in me? The demon took over and decided he didn't like Doyle. I don't always remember what he does when he's in control. He's powerful."

"You've gone to the worst possibility first," I said. "I'm sure something else is going on. And yes, we have seen your demon side in action, and he's tricky, but there'll be another explanation."

"Are you able to sit up?" Zandra asked Finn. "You might feel better. I'll get you some water."

"I can. But I need help. I may have busted a rib or two."

I climbed off Finn, and Zandra assisted him into a seated position, so his back was against the door. He almost passed out from the effort but seemed more comfortable after a few minutes. I headed to the sink with Zandra. "I'll examine Doyle's body and look around the scene. It's a chaotic mess in there, so Finn could have missed something important. A clue as to who did this."

Zandra nodded. "There must have been someone else here. Someone who attacked them."

"Few people know about Doyle being in Crimson Cove," I said, "or his connection to Finn."

"They weren't exactly low-key when they were in town," Zandra said. "Maybe someone recognized Doyle and remembered an old grudge."

"I'll see if I can find anything useful." I jumped down from the kitchen counter and headed back to the crime scene. The stench was overwhelming, and I had to take shallow breaths as my stomach turned over. I'd seen my fair share of crime scenes since moving to Crimson Cove, but this one had to be the worst. There was evidence of violence, pain, and trauma everywhere my gaze settled.

I returned to Doyle's body and, with a dispassionate eye, inspected it. One wing had been burned down to the nub, and there were injuries on his arms suggesting he'd attempted to protect himself from the flames. There were also burn marks on the walls, going as high as the ceiling. The flames must have burned hot and violently.

Everything was so badly burned, it was impossible to tell if there was anything odd about the scene, so I returned to the kitchen. "Finn, I know this won't be pleasant, but can you come to the room where the fight happened? You may notice something I've missed. You're more familiar with the room's layout than we are."

He grimaced but slowly hauled himself up with Zandra's help. "I'll do it. I have to find out how this happened."

"Don't automatically think you did it." Zandra guided him slowly toward the room. "The attacker could have snuck in while you were talking to Doyle and you didn't hear them until it was too late."

"But why do this?" Finn gestured at the fire-seared room, his face pale and sweaty from the effort of moving.

"Demons aren't often the good guys," I said. "Maybe there's something in Doyle's past that reared up when he came to Crimson Cove."

"This was his first visit to town," Finn said. "He told me that last night."

"Let's take a look and go from there," I said.

Finn inched his way into the room, assisted by Zandra. He stopped moving, and a single tear trickled down his cheek. "I wish I could remember what happened, but it's just a blank."

"We'll get your head injury checked out as soon as we can," Zandra said. "Maybe you'll get your memories back and remember someone else being here."

"Yeah, maybe." Finn didn't sound too certain, though.

We'd just begun our visual inspection of the room when there was a pounding on the front door.

I hurried to the window and looked out, my hackles lifting and my stomach flip-flopping. "We've got trouble. It's Cythera and Bertoli."

Chapter 5

Time's up

"Don't let them in!" Finn whispered urgently then staggered away.

"We can't pretend we're not here," I said.

"How do they even know about this?" Zandra peeked around the side of the door as a fist thudded against the main door again.

"Maybe a neighbor smelled the smoke." I glanced back into the room. The scene suggested the fight had happened a while ago, though. Doyle was cold, and there was no smoke lingering.

"Someone could have heard the fight and they've only just reported it," Zandra said. "Things have been smashed, and there are holes in the walls. That would have made a noise."

I wrinkled my booping snooter. Something felt wrong. "A violent fight would have been reported straight away, no matter the time it happened, so why are the angels only showing up now? I know they love a long coffee break, but this is ridiculous."

Zandra arched an eyebrow. "An all-night break? Even Finn's coffee breaks aren't that long."

"To find out why they've been delayed, we'll have to open the door and ask them," I said. "But from the increasingly loud thuds, that option may soon be out of our paws."

"I can't let them take me in." Finn raked his hands through his sooty hair. "They'll take one look at this place and think I'm guilty of murder."

Zandra stepped into his path and caught hold of his shoulders. "Cythera knows you."

"And she doesn't like what she knows!"

"She does. She just has a tough time showing it," I said. "The more critical she is of a person, the more she admires them."

"Nice try, Juno, but that's not true." Finn gulped in air. "We could hide the body, just until I remember what happened."

I winced. "That would make you look guilty. We know you didn't do it. You wouldn't have sent us a message if you did this. You'd be too busy concealing evidence."

"If I were investigating this case, I'd look at the scene and blame me," Finn said.

"At first glance, perhaps. But we've worked together for a long time now, and we know your reputation. So does Cythera. Zandra, open the door," I said.

Zandra nodded at Finn and squeezed his shoulders. "We've got your back. If Cythera gets any dumb ideas, we'll protect you. Keep saying you're innocent until we work out who did this."

He heaved out a sigh, his shoulders rounding. "Go let them in."

Zandra strode to the door and opened it. Surprise flashed across Cythera's face when she saw her. "What are you doing here?"

I joined Zandra. "Don't be quick to jump to any conclusions. Things aren't what they seem."

Cythera's gaze cut over Zandra's head, and disappointment flickered in her eyes. "Finn. I really didn't want to find you here."

Finn's shoulders sagged even more. "I can explain. At least, some of it."

"Let's get this over with." Cythera stepped inside, and Bertoli followed her, nodding at us, his expression grim.

"There's a body in here?" Cythera asked Finn.

His eyebrows flashed up, but he nodded. "This way. Watch out. There's a mess." Finn led them into the room where Doyle had met his fiery end, and we followed closely behind.

Cythera and Bertoli stood in the doorway for a full minute, neither of them speaking as they surveyed the devastation.

"This is your handiwork?" Cythera finally said to Finn, her tone tight.

"I... I don't know."

"This has nothing to do with him," I said. "Finn and Doyle were assaulted. Look at Finn's head injury. We need to find their attacker."

"There was someone else here?" Bertoli asked.

"Maybe. I don't remember," Finn said. "I came to in this room and found the place on fire. I thought my dad was injured at first. But then..." He gestured at the body.

"This man was your father?" Cythera pointed at the charred body. "I didn't think you had one."

"Everyone has a father," I said, "although some don't always step up to their responsibilities. Doyle and his friends arrived in Crimson Cove yesterday. He claimed to be Finn's biological father."

"He is! At least he was. He knew things about me. Things no one else could," Finn said.

Cythera's forehead wrinkled. She looked at us. "Why are you here? You still haven't told me."

"Finn sent us a message," Zandra said cautiously.

"He asked you to come and clear up his mess? Hide the evidence?" Her wings fluttered.

"No! Finn was panicked and confused. Look at his head. The concussion is most likely affecting his memory," I said.

"Sending you a message rather than reporting this crime as soon as possible suggests he's involved," Cythera said. "And then to recruit close friends to get him out of trouble—"

"I wasn't thinking straight," Finn said. "I had a terrible headache, and it took me a while to realize where I was and what I'd been doing. And I've got blanks in my memory." He gestured at us. "I pulled out my mobile globe and brought up the last number I'd used and sent a message. I was fortunate it was Zandra, not the local takeout."

"You should have contacted me," Cythera said. "A serious crime has been committed here."

"We see that," I said cooly. "And Finn is an innocent victim in the crime, not the criminal. Why would he murder his alleged father when they were just getting to know each other?"

"I can think of half a dozen reasons," Cythera said.

Finn inspected his damaged hands and grimaced. "This looks bad for me, but I was excited about meeting Doyle. We were making plans. Doyle's done well for himself, and he wanted to know more about the animal sanctuary. He said he was thinking of making a donation and getting involved."

Cythera drew in a deep breath, her nose wrinkling at the unpleasant odors lingering in the air. "Everyone, stay out of the way while we examine the scene. Finn, don't go anywhere and touch nothing."

"Sure. I know the protocol. I'll stay back with Zandra and Juno."

"Bertoli, stay with them," Cythera said. "Make sure they behave."

He nodded, his expression tight.

"I won't run!" Finn said.

"I'm taking no chances."

While Cythera conducted a preliminary sweep of the room, I pulled Bertoli to one side. "Congratulations on passing your sergeant's exam." He had a small, gleaming silver star pinned to his lapel to show his newly promoted rank.

"Thanks, Juno. I didn't think my first case as a sergeant would be this, though."

"How did you know there was trouble at this house?" I asked.

Bertoli pressed his lips together. "An eyewitness came in first thing this morning in a panic. It took us a while to get any sense out of him. He babbled about an angel and a demon fighting, and fire, and chaos. We thought he was hallucinating."

"An eyewitness saw what happened? That's excellent news. They must have seen the killer."

"Unfortunately, they did," Bertoli said. "They were passing the house after hiking all day. It was late when they saw a flash of light through the window. The eyewitness took a look and saw a fight."

"So you know who the attacker is?"

Bertoli closed his eyes for a second and pinched the bridge of his nose. "He described Finn perfectly."

My heart sank. "The eyewitness saw Finn kill Doyle?"

Bertoli nodded. "Finn is in big trouble, and I'm not sure how he's getting out of it."

"If the fight happened late last night, why did the eyewitness only inform you this morning?" Zandra asked. "If I saw a fight between an angel and a demon, I'd step in to stop it or report it straight away."

"The eyewitness said he panicked. He was scared that he'd been seen and someone would come after him. He intended to leave Crimson Cove, but since it was so late, he set up camp nearby. He said he didn't sleep a wink thinking about it, so as soon as it got light, he walked back into town and reported the crime to us."

"I've seen enough." Cythera walked over to Finn. "I don't want to cuff you, but I will if you make things difficult."

"Cuff him!" I strode over. "This is premature."

Finn lowered his head. "I won't put up a fight. I don't remember harming Doyle, but I must have been involved."

"Say nothing else," I said. "You're innocent. Everyone knows that."

Finn shrugged and kept his head down.

"I've called this into headquarters," Cythera said. "They're sending Brodie."

"Who's Brodie?" Zandra asked.

"My worst nightmare," Finn muttered. "If he's involved in my sentencing, my life is officially over."

***

After the devastating discovery at the house, Cythera and Bertoli took Finn to Angel Force. We'd wanted to go with them, but Cythera said she'd give us an update as soon as she had news, and there was paperwork to be done before any interviews took place. So we headed to Sorcha's café to wait for an update.

I was so worried about Finn that I could barely eat my second breakfast of scrambled eggs. Even Sammy's comforting presence wasn't enough to soothe my concern.

Sorcha came over and settled in a seat opposite us once she'd served a customer. She brought a fresh plate of blueberry muffins and snacks for me and Sammy.

"I don't enjoy gossiping about a friend," she whispered, "but how did this happen?"

"That's the mystery," Zandra said. "Finn believes both front and back doors were locked, and it was only the two of them inside the house."

Sorcha shook her head. "The rumors are spreading fast that an angel's been arrested for a terrible crime, but I'm stunned Finn could be involved. There must be a mistake."

"It's good to know Crimson Cove's gossip grapevine is operating at full strength when one of their own is in trouble," I grumbled.

"Finn would never do anything so bad," Sammy said. "He's a decent guy. He's a friend to the animals, so he gets my vote for being innocent."

"We all think he's innocent," Zandra said, "but if you'd seen that room where we found the body, you may have had cause to doubt. It was a mess."

I sampled a small piece of egg. "And we have to assume Doyle was a powerful demon, since we've all seen Finn in action when his demon side takes over. It would have been hard to bring Doyle down."

"Do you know anything about the eyewitness who reported the crime?" Sorcha asked.

"Bertoli didn't give us many details, but I know it's a male who was hiking through Crimson Cove." I sniffed the dried meat stick Sorcha gave me, but I couldn't face more food, so pushed it over to Sammy.

"This witness must be reliable if the angels trust his statement," Sorcha said. She looked up as the door opened, and several customers entered. "Be back in a minute."

"You'll figure this out," Sammy said. "You never let your friends down. You stood by me when I was in trouble."

"Of course. We'll always do that," I said.

"We need Finn to remember what actually happened," Zandra said. "Otherwise, we're stuck with a mess of evidence pointing to his guilt."

I looked over at the counter, and my eyes widened. "Those are Doyle's friends! The two guys we met in the pizza parlor yesterday."

Zandra turned in her seat, and we watched as Carlito and Bael grabbed takeout food. They were in and out within two minutes.

"They don't seem sad," Zandra said.

"Maybe they don't know what happened to Doyle," I said.

"Or they're glad he's dead."

"Do you want me to speak to them?" A sparkle of magic shimmered across Sammy's glossy fur.

I briefly leaned against him. "No need. We should follow them to see where they go."

"You're leaving?" Sorcha hurried back to the table as we stood. "Have you had news from Angel Force?"

"No, but we're following some leads," I said. "We'll let you know as soon as we hear anything."

With a quick goodbye to Sammy and Sorcha, we dashed out of the café. We tracked Bael and Carlito to the edge of town. They weren't in a hurry, and as they ate their food, they were laughing and joking with each other as they sauntered along.

"They hardly seem to be grieving," Zandra said.

"I agree. They look more like they're celebrating."

"Angel Force must have contacted them about Doyle."

"Unless they don't know they're connected to him," I said.

"I figured they were all staying in the same house," Zandra said. "It's big enough. The angels would have sealed it off until they finished their investigation. They must have been back and seen what was going on."

"Unless a guilty conscience is keeping them away. Let's keep watching them, see what they do," I said.

Our discreet tracking led us to Torrin Connors' repair garage. Instead of going in, they glided past and entered the bar next door.

"Day drinking," I murmured. "Could they be doing it because they're sad or because they're feeling joyful?"

"We need to go in and ask them." Magic flickered on Zandra's fingers.

I hopped onto her shoulder. "Keep your anger in check. We won't stop searching until we find the killer, but if you go in all magic flaring, we'll end up in a fight and get no answers."

She took a couple of deep breaths. "I hate the thought of Finn being stuck in a cell, not knowing what happened and thinking he lost control. It makes me sick."

"Me, too. Which is why we keep a level head before the obliteration begins. Got it?"

Zandra kissed my side. "Got it."

We waited until they'd gone inside and then followed. As expected at this time of day, the bar was quiet, with only a few people around, most of them with mugs of coffee or finishing a late breakfast.

"They could be meeting Doyle's other friends," I said. "The two women who showed up at the pizza parlor. Maybe they're all in on this. They wanted Doyle dead and recognized Finn as the perfect fall guy. They sneaked into the house, murdered Doyle, and set Finn up."

"It's a possibility, but let's not get ahead of ourselves," Zandra said.

"It's time for a fake meeting," I said. "Let's go to the bar and order while accidentally bumping into our new acquaintances."

We strolled over, standing close to Carlito and Bael, and Zandra thumped around the menus and deliberately knocked over a salt shaker.

Bael glanced our way. "Hey! I know you. You're Finn's friends."

"Greetings! I'm happy to say we are," I said. "And you're Bael and Carlito."

Carlito flicked a glare at us. "You need to pick better friends."

"Oh! You know what's going on?" Zandra asked.

"Of course we do. I knew there was something off with that guy the second I met him," Carlito said.

"You mean Finn?" I asked.

"Who else? Murdered our buddy just for kicks. Stinkin' hybrid freak."

I gently dug my claws into Zandra's shoulder as she tensed. "Who told you what happened?"

"We got contacted by some snooty angel. She wanted to know if we'd seen anything weird going on at the house last night," Bael said.

"And did you?" I asked.

"We weren't there," Carlito said.

"Where were you?"

"Elsewhere."

"We're sorry for your loss." Zandra's voice was level, even though her heartbeat had sped up. "Had you known Doyle long?"

Bael shrugged. "Sure."

"Are you planning on sticking around Crimson Cove until the angels figure out what happened?" I asked.

"No," Carlito said.

"We should. See if the angels let that jerk loose. Then we can teach him some manners." Bael cracked his knuckles, and a flicker of red demon energy shifted down his body.

"Do you know anyone who wanted to mess with Doyle?" I asked. "Perhaps someone he knew who lived here?"

"Can't say we do." Carlito turned his back to us. "We're busy."

"Doing what?" Zandra asked. "We can join you for drinks, maybe figure out what happened to Doyle."

"We're busy not talking to you. We don't talk to demon hunters who have hybrid freak killers as friends," Carlito said.

Their drinks arrived, and they headed to the back of the bar, muttering to each other and shooting glares our way.

"That went well," Zandra muttered.

"They didn't want to talk to us," I said.

"Worried they'll let something slip and make themselves look guilty?"

I glowered at them as I nodded. "They're hiding things from us, and I intend to find out why."

Chapter 6

Big trouble

"Cythera must be worried if she's keeping us informed about what's going on." I sat on Zandra's shoulder as she hurried to Angel Force. She'd received a short message from Cythera less than ten minutes ago, letting us know Finn had been processed and was in a cell. And he was about to be interviewed.

"I guess so. Although it wasn't exactly an open invitation for us to get involved," Zandra said.

"But we're doing so."

"Of course. Finn's our friend, and he's in serious trouble. Everyone can sense it."

"There must have been another person involved," I said. "Or the eyewitness made a mistake. He could have seen Doyle fighting with an angel, but it wasn't Finn."

"Do you know any other angels who have the ability to blast out demon flames?" Zandra asked. "I'm not saying that because I think Finn's guilty, but I've not met another angel like him, and I don't think there are any other angel-demons living in Crimson Cove."

"Then Finn was fighting his father's attacker," I said. "This eyewitness saw Finn in a struggle with a demon, but it wasn't his dad. Maybe Doyle was already dead, and the body was missed because the eyewitness was watching the fight."

"It's hard to miss a flaming body on the floor, but it's a possibility." Zandra pulled open the main doors to Angel Force and strode through the reception area. "Whatever happens, Finn will soon be a free angel."

The atmosphere in the open-plan office radiated with tension. Angels hurried around doing their usual work, but they looked tense and miserable. Finn was popular, and his arrest would have hit his colleagues hard.

Bertoli raised a hand when he saw us and stood from his desk. "Has Cythera brought you up to speed?"

"Not really. She sent a message to say Finn was about to be interviewed, though," Zandra said.

"By Brodie. He's one of our warrior angels. He's fought in over ten wars and has so many medals, he can't carry them on both wings when they're outstretched. He retired from active duty and now trains new recruits at the Academy." Bertoli inclined his head toward Cythera's office. "Brodie arrived a few minutes ago and has been in there ever since getting info on the case."

I examined the huge angel standing in front of Cythera's desk. He had his back to us, but I could tell he had an enormous wingspan with steel tips on his wings and a scar running across the back of his shaven head.

He shifted his head a fraction as if sensing he was being watched and glanced at us from the corner of his eye before returning his attention to Cythera.

"Brodie has a seriously impressive reputation." There was a hint of awe in Bertoli's voice. "And he takes no prisoners. He's not your typical angel. Warrior angels are a breed apart. We're known for our benevolence and kind heart. They're not."

"Is that so?" I flicked an ear. "Perhaps you'd be better suited as a warrior angel?"

Bertoli's cheeks flushed scarlet. "I'll admit, I was a giant jerk to you when you first arrived in Crimson Cove, but I hope you can see I've changed. I'm working hard to be a better angel."

"You're doing great," Zandra said. "Juno's teasing. How's Finn doing?"

Bertoli grimaced. "He's a mess. Do you want to see him? He'd appreciate a friendly face or two."

"Take us to him," I said.

Bertoli led us to the cells and along the corridor to where Finn had been placed. He was slumped on the floor, his knees up and head down.

"You've got visitors," Bertoli said.

Finn glanced up, the misery on his face tugging at my heart.

"Do you need anything?" Bertoli asked.

Finn shook his head. "I'm good. Thanks."

Bertoli appeared torn between wanting to stay and getting away as fast as he could.

"We'll take it from here," I said gently.

He nodded and hurried away, leaving us alone. The other cells were empty, so we were free to talk.

"Has Cythera been treating you well?" Zandra asked.

"She's been great. She keeps reassuring me that she'll do what she can, but I can tell she's concerned about what was found at the house."

"The angels must have processed the crime scene by now," I said. "Any updates?"

"Not that I've been told. I guess they've moved Doyle by now and will start the autopsy."

"Most likely," Zandra said. "And they won't be slow about running tests and figuring out what happened. Once they do, they'll know you weren't involved."

Finn rubbed his forehead with the tips of his fingers. "I wish I could remember. But I have a big blank at the most important moment."

"It'll come back," Zandra said. "Has a doctor checked you?"

Finn nodded. "No concussion, and I had healing magic for the injuries." He held up his hands to show they were burn-free. "I don't feel like I deserve it, though. Not if I did that to my dad."

"Finn, this may not be the right time to bring this up, but are you certain that man was your biological father?" I asked.

Finn narrowed his eyes at me then, with a sigh, he deflated. "I was suspicious at first, too. He got in touch with me about a month ago. He sent a message to say we had a connection, and he'd like to meet. I ignored it at first. After all, you know my background. My childhood wasn't all sunshine and rainbows. But he persisted. Doyle said he'd changed. He deeply regretted abandoning me, but he'd had no choice."

"When we met him, Doyle mentioned he went through tough times," Zandra said. "Did he tell you what they were?"

"He hinted at a few things. He spent time with some shady demons, and they were running around and getting themselves in trouble," Finn said. "I looked Doyle up on the system, and he's got a record. Mainly acts of violence. He ran with crowds who worked a racketeering ring, extorting money from businesses. He's even served time inside."

"Why would you want to get to know someone like that?" I asked.

"Because he's changed! He hasn't committed a crime in over thirty years."

"Perhaps he has, but he hasn't been caught," I said cautiously.

Finn raked a hand through his hair. "I know! And I'm not an idiot, but I got interested in what he had to tell me. I wanted to know where I came from. Doyle said he'd reformed and turned his life around. He'd set up a magic spell recycling company that takes the emissions from demon magic and does something to them. I got overwhelmed with the details. It's cutting-edge stuff, mixing science and magic. He was planning to franchise the business and make a fortune."

"Sounds impressive," I said.

"Doyle was excited about it," Finn said. "And once he'd cleaned up his act, he wanted to fix things from his past. Things he badly messed up."

"So, he found you and wanted to make amends?" Zandra asked.

Finn nodded. "I thought it was too good to be true and questioned him for hours the first time we met."

"Is that why you went missing?" I asked.

"Yeah. Sorry for dropping off the planet for a couple of days, but Doyle wanted us to spend quality time together and get to know each other. We went on a wild camping trip. Well, it was super fancy and loaded with luxurious food and drink, but it was just the two of us in this huge, glamping-style yurt. We went on long hikes, cooked together, and talked for hours. He was legit. And sure, Doyle had a few rough edges, but who hasn't?"

"And then you brought him to Crimson Cove to show him your life?" I asked.

"Doyle said he wanted to see every aspect of my world. And since working at Angel Force is such a big part of it, I decided to show him around. I wanted him to see the animal sanctuary, too. I'm so proud of that place. And I wanted him to meet my friends." Finn's smile was tinged with tiredness. "You all mean so much to me. When I've messed up in the past, you've always been there to dig me out of the hole."

"And we're still here," I said. "We won't stop digging until you're free."

"When Cythera told you Brodie would look after your case, you didn't seem happy about it," Zandra said. "Do we have a problem with him?"

Finn tipped his head back and stared at the ceiling. "Unfortunately, we do. Brodie was brought into the Academy as an instructor, specifically to work with angel hybrids. The Academy wanted to ensure we could be trusted in such responsible roles. And they tested us to the limits. Or rather, Brodie tested our limits. Half the squad I was in dropped out because he was so rough on them."

"Why would he do that?" Zandra asked.

"When they first opened Angel Force to hybrids, there was a suspicion that we couldn't be relied upon. They put us through our paces to make sure we didn't mess up and go rogue. They didn't want Angel Force's glowing reputation sullied."

I scowled. "The angels are such a cautious bunch. You make an excellent law enforcer. You're the best this place has."

"Brodie hated me," Finn said. "I talked back to him, and I questioned his orders. I don't think he was used to that."

"I didn't hate you, but you sure were a pain in my butt at times."

I jumped at the sound of the surly voice at the end of the corridor. Somehow, Brodie had crept inside. His face was almost as scarred as the back of his head, with a long-healed wound running from one eye down to his chin. His eyes were ice blue and focused on Finn as he strode toward us, all menacing, loaded muscle, and confidence. The kind of confidence you only get if you're certain you're an alpha and no one has disputed that for a long time. Maybe never.

"I never tolerate disrespect." Brodie stopped by the cell, his gaze locked onto Finn. "And you used to give it to me in bucketfuls."

The two men stared at each other, unblinking.

"I was never disrespectful, but when I didn't agree with your orders or wanted extra information, I asked for it," Finn said.

Brodie grunted. "You had a smart mouth, but you were a fast learner. I'm disappointed to see you in this situation."

"Same here," Finn said.

"Greetings," I said. "I'm—"

"I know who you are. Cythera filled me in." Brodie didn't take his eyes off Finn. "I'll be fair to you if you're honest with me."

"I have no reason to lie about anything," Finn said. "Let's just get this over with."

"The interview room is ready," Brodie said. "I'll be leading."

"Sure. Whatever you think best." Finn stood slowly. "Juno and Zandra are representing me, so I want them in on the interviews. Mine and any witnesses or other suspects you bring in."

Brodie flicked a glance our way, a whisper of curiosity in his cold eyes. "You sure? They're trained legal professionals?"

"They have my back. And they won't let me down," Finn said.

Brodie shrugged. "I have no issue with that. Pick who you like." He unlocked the cell door, and Finn stepped out.

I rested a paw on his shoulder. "We'll do everything we can to make this right. We know you, Finn, and you'd never do this."

"Keep up," Brodie said as he strode away.

We followed Brodie back into the open-plan office and into a small private interview room.

Bertoli was already in there, a notepad in front of him. He gifted Finn a reassuring smile, although it was littered with concern.

Brodie took the seat next to Bertoli and waited for Finn and Zandra to settle into seats. I sat on Zandra's lap and studied Brodie. He came across as a no-nonsense angel, someone you wouldn't want to meet in a dark alley when committing a murky deed, but I didn't detect malice in him. Still, I'd watch him like a hawk to ensure he behaved professionally and had no issue with Finn. If I detected an ounce of bias, my murder mittens would fly free and I'd give Brodie new scars to add to his collection.

Brodie ran through the formalities before starting his questioning.

"Talk me through what happened that evening," Brodie said.

"There's not much to tell," Finn said. "I had pizza with Doyle and his friends. Zandra and Juno were there for a while, then I went back to the rental Doyle was staying in while he was here. We had more to drink and talked for a while."

"Do we have the friends' details?" Brodie glanced at Bertoli.

He nodded. "They've been contacted."

"Good. I'll want to interview them, too." Brodie looked back at Finn. "What did you talk about?"

"Everything and anything. Doyle told me more about his business and his plans for the future, and I talked about living in Crimson Cove and working at Angel Force. I told him more about my friends here and the animal sanctuary I run. We were getting to know each other."

"Did you fight?"

Finn hesitated. "We disagreed over a few things."

"Such as?"

Finn glanced away. "I pushed Doyle to find out why he abandoned me when I was a kid. He wasn't with my mother for long, and they were in a bad place when I arrived. I understand why they gave me up, but I wanted to know why he didn't try harder to turn things around so he could keep me. Wasn't I worth fighting for? Wasn't I a good enough reason for him to get his head on straight?"

"That's a big issue to resolve with one conversation," Brodie said.

"We'd only just scratched the surface."

"And then what? You talked. Argued. And..."

"I remember feeling tired. It had been a long day, and Doyle was a full-on guy. He had so much energy and was always on the go. I was thinking about calling it a night, and that's the last thing I remember. There's just a blank. I woke up to fire and blood."

"Was there anyone else with you?" Brodie asked.

Finn shook his head.

"What about Doyle's friends? Weren't they with you?"

"No, they were off doing their own thing," Finn said. "We wanted bonding time together, just the two of us."

"How do you know for sure they weren't there if you've got a blank in your memory?"

Finn closed his eyes for a second. "I don't, not really. I suppose someone could have come in, but if they did, I have no recollection of that."

Brodie huffed out a breath and sat back in his seat, crossing his arms over his chest. "I'll be frank with you. We've run initial tests at the crime scene. The flames that killed Doyle were supernatural."

Finn swallowed. "I figured as much. You don't kill a demon with regular fire."

"Agreed. So, do you know anyone around here who has a habit of turning into a psycho demon when he gets angry?" Brodie asked.

Nobody spoke, and a lump of churning worry formed in my gut. Finn was in so much trouble.

Chapter 7

Tough times

Brodie grilled Finn for another half-hour, basically asking the same question, but in different ways. Each time, Finn told him the same story. He couldn't remember what had happened at the house. He didn't know if anyone else had been there, and he didn't see anyone attack his dad. He never slipped up or changed the details. Clearly frustrated, Brodie returned Finn to his cell.

I waited with Zandra in Cythera's office, along with Bertoli and Cythera. None of us wore happy expressions.

Brodie strolled in and shut the door behind him. "You've got a stubborn one there."

"Maybe a truthful one," I said. "No matter how many times you asked Finn, he told you the exact same thing. That's because he's telling you the truth."

Brodie stretched his back, rubbing his knuckles into the base of his spine. "He's good. But they always make a mistake, eventually. Give me enough time, and he'll get his memory back." He said the last words using air quotes.

"What if he doesn't have a memory to retrieve?" Zandra rested her hands on her hips. "Finn was injured. When we found him in the house, he was unconscious."

"He needed significant healing magic once we'd brought him in," Cythera said.

"Maybe it was self-inflicted," Brodie said. "He wanted to make sure the finger of suspicion wasn't pointed at him. The simplest way to do that was to hurt himself. Or Finn fought with Doyle. They got into it, and Doyle landed a blow before Finn incinerated him."

"No!" all four of us said at the same time.

Brodie looked momentarily startled, then he smirked. "It's understandable why you're all defending him. That's why I'm here. You all know, like, or work with Finn. That makes you impartial and useless to this investigation."

"We need to be here to make sure no injustice is done," I said. "The way you're talking, you've already decided he's guilty."

"I decide innocence or guilt based on the evidence presented to me," Brodie replied. "I'll focus on the facts, not some fantasy about a mysterious intruder no one saw. Including the eyewitness, who gave a detailed description of Doyle's killer. It was a perfect match for Finn."

Cythera tugged at one wing. "That's true, but it was very late, and the eyewitness said he was tired. Tired eyes play tricks."

"And that trick put Finn at the murder scene," I said.

Brodie blew out a breath. "It's only natural you want to defend him and find evidence of his innocence. I get that. And I won't only look for facts that point to his guilt. I'm open to all interpretations. But if Finn is guilty, he's going down for this crime."

We all scowled at Brodie, and his logic frustrated me. He made an annoyingly accurate point, though. He had to look at the evidence, and unfortunately, it was pointing the finger of guilt directly at Finn.

But we wouldn't give up. It was so out of character, and Finn had been happy and proud when he'd introduced us to Doyle. I refused to believe that things had changed so drastically in such a short amount of time.

"I need a break," Brodie said. "Where's good around here for a burger?"

"Are you taking time off already?" Zandra asked. "You've only just gotten started."

"A guy needs to eat. Questioning people always makes me hungry."

"We'll show you around," I said. "We have a great pizza place."

He shook his head. "I'm not in the mood for pizza. I want a big hunk of meat."

"Sorcha's café?" Zandra looked at me.

"How about the bar? They do a good burger there."

"Sounds like my kind of place," Brodie said.

I nodded my satisfaction. We could take Brodie there and see if Doyle's tight-lipped demon friends were still around. We'd introduce them to Brodie and see if he could shake answers out of them. At the very least, we could show him there were plenty of other suspects to interrogate, rather than focusing on Finn.

Maverick appeared in the open-plan office, a huge box in his hands. He called out a greeting to everyone.

Cythera grimaced. "Please, no more wedding paraphernalia. There's no time to make changes now, but he keeps on prodding things and making adjustments."

"Roll with it," I said. "That's how Maverick is. He wants your special day to be one-of-a-kind."

"It will be. And at this rate, I'll be remembering it for all the wrong reasons." She waved a hand at us. "Go. There's nothing more we can do right now for Finn."

Maverick appeared by the office door and smiled warmly. "I have urgent questions, my love. Can you spare me a few minutes?"

"Come in. But make it quick. I've got lots to do," Cythera said.

"Good luck," I whispered to Maverick as we passed him.

Brodie strolled out of the building and stood in silence for a moment, looking around. "Where's the bar?"

"On the edge of town. They have a late license, so they're out of the way of the houses to avoid getting noise complaints. Follow us," I said.

He fell into step with Zandra and me, looking at the different stores we passed.

"Bertoli told us you fought in a number of angel wars," I said.

"That's right."

"But now you're retired?"

"I don't do this for the love of it. I work part-time for Angel Force and freelance as a consultant for anyone who can afford me."

"Doing what?" Zandra asked.

"The kind of jobs most angels don't touch." Brodie swept his steel-tipped wings through the air. "Not all angels like to get their hands dirty."

"Are you an assassin for the angels?" I asked.

He smirked. "If I was, I wouldn't tell you. You don't need the details, but Angel Force comes to me when they need someone bad taken down."

"I hope you don't include Finn on that list of bad people," I said. "He's the best angel Cythera has. He took a lot of flak when he started working in Crimson Cove because he was one of the first angel hybrids to join the team. He stuck it out, even when there was so much prejudice against him. Speaks a lot about his character."

"You'll hear no arguments against that statement from me," Brodie said. "But there's something you need to know about Finn."

"What's that?" Zandra asked.

"Angel Force has a watchlist. Names go on it when they have concerns about people they employ."

I hissed softly. "Let me guess, every name on the list is an angel hybrid?"

Brodie shrugged. "For all the goodness we're supposed to be full of, we have some weirdly old-fashioned prejudices lingering. You won't find any of that from me, though. I've seen enough of the world to know things don't operate in a fluffy white bubble of pureness. There are shades of gray in everyone. But the powers that be at the top of Angel Force were reluctant to open the doors of law enforcement to magical muddles."

"So they keep this watchlist to check up on them?" Zandra looked at me. "That's unfair. It's like they've tarred and feathered them before they've even put a foot wrong."

"Yeah, it sucks. But Finn's name is close to the top of that list. There have been reports that he's let his demon side slip out once too often."

I scowled as I stamped along. I'd seen Finn's demon side in action more than once, and it was a scarily powerful thing, but he'd always gotten it under control with a little help from his friends.

"I don't expect either of you to go telling tales about Finn if he's struggling," Brodie said.

"We have no tales to tell," I said sharply. "Finn is excellent at what he does."

"I'd expect you to say nothing less. And I appreciate you standing up for a friend. Loyalty is an excellent trait. But don't interfere with this investigation if you know he's guilty."

"We know nothing about what happened that night," Zandra said. "We weren't there. Other than Doyle and Finn, no one knows what happened."

"The killer does," I said. "And it's not Finn."

"You think the eyewitness is lying?" Brodie asked.

"As Cythera said, eyewitnesses aren't always reliable," I said. "It would be good to meet him face-to-face and examine his character."

Brodie chuckled. "Sure, it would. I've heard about you, Juno. You're likely to threaten to obliterate him until he takes back his statement."

"I never obliterate unless absolutely necessary," I said. "But we must be able to speak to the eyewitness. Finn's guilt or innocence rests upon this one person's statement."

"The statement has value, but there's physical evidence, too. They were the only two in the house. Finn is more than capable of producing demon flames, and they were both injured by fire."

"But why would Finn kill Doyle?" Zandra asked. "They were getting along so well."

"Demons have quick tempers and behave impulsively," Brodie said. "You must know this. Crypt witches are famous for their dealings with demons. I've even been to Willow Tree Falls and dropped off convicted criminals who'll be spending eternity in the prison below the cemetery."

"Demons have their... well, demons to deal with, but Finn and Doyle were in a good place. They were happy to be with each other. I've never seen Finn so happy," I said.

"Well, he's not happy now, so something went badly wrong." Brodie lifted his chin toward a neon sign on the outside of the bar as we approached. "Is this the place?"

Zandra nodded. "It has the best burgers in town. And it won't be busy at this time of day."

"And you never know who you might meet in here," I said.

Brodie shot me a curious look but didn't ask a question as we headed into the quiet bar. Music was playing from the sound system, and there were a dozen occupied tables with diners or early afternoon drinkers.

I looked around for any signs of Bael or Carlito. Zandra nodded at me and herded Brodie toward the bar, giving me time to look. I hurried to the booth where I'd last seen them. It was empty. A quick hunt around left me disappointed. They were nowhere to be seen. We must have missed them.

While Brodie was placing his order, I gestured to an unfamiliar face working behind the bar. She was young, in her mid-twenties, with streaks of purple hair, and an ivy tattoo running down the side of her face that extended down her neck and disappeared below her T-shirt collar.

"What'll it be, cutie?" she asked.

"Greetings! I haven't seen you here before."

"I'm Glade. Just started working here. Well, just moved to Crimson Cove, actually. This is the first job I found." She raised her eyebrows as she waited for my order.

"Welcome. You'll find it a fascinating area. My wonderful witch is placing our order, but I have a question about some of your customers. Two demons. Go by the names of Carlito and Bael. They were here earlier and took that booth at the back. Do you remember them?"

She nodded. "Sure. They stayed for a few rounds."

"Did you overhear any of their conversation?"

She narrowed her eyes a fraction. "Are they in trouble?"

"Potentially. They're connected to a recent murder victim."

"Oh! And how are you involved in something so nasty?"

"I work with the angels on their most perplexing cases. The prime suspect is a good friend of mine, and I'm determined to ensure he doesn't go down for a crime he didn't commit."

Glade nodded along as I spoke. "Well, I didn't overhear anything they talked about. If you want to speak to them, they left about thirty minutes ago. They were talking about hiring a boat to go sea fishing. Is that a thing around here?"

"We have a wonderful pebble beach a short walk from the town. And I believe you can hire boats there. When are they going sailing?"

"They didn't say, but I figured they were heading straight there. If you hurry, you may catch them before they leave." Glade shuddered. "Not a fan of the sea, myself. You never know what's lurking beneath those waves with big teeth and an empty stomach."

"I'm in agreement with you there. And the saltwater does nothing for my fur. Thanks for the information."

She nodded at me. "Anytime."

I dashed back to Zandra just as Brodie strolled away. "Where's he off to?"

"Restroom. Did you find them?"

"We're too late. But I know where they're going. They want to try sea fishing."

Zandra grimaced. "And let me guess, you want to go to the beach?"

"I hope you've got your sea legs ready."

Chapter 8

Fishy surprise

After making excuses with Brodie, who seemed happy we were leaving him alone so he could enjoy his burger in peace, we hurried to the pebble beach. It was a pleasant enough day, so several people were enjoying walks with their familiars.

We sped along the beach until we reached a row of small huts. Some were used as pop-up stores to sell treats to visitors, while a few were rented out to day-trippers, and the rest were permanent stores. One of the huts was set up as a boat and scuba gear rental place.

I headed inside with Zandra, wrinkling my booping snooter at the smell of saltwater and the pungent, meaty aroma of fish food. I didn't look closely at the buckets of wriggling critters being sold to the fishermen. They always turned my stomach.

The store had a maritime theme, with a blue and white color scheme, several wooden seagulls dotted around, and a fishing net tacked onto one wall.

A guy with a long, white beard and a bald head stood behind the counter. He was a grizzled old warlock of indeterminate age, but he had warm blue eyes.

"Fishing or scuba-diving?" he asked as we approached the counter.

"Boat hire," Zandra said. "We're looking for two demons who just hired a boat to go sea fishing."

"Oh, those two," he said. "With them, are you?"

"No, we're definitely not," I said and made the introductions.

He nodded. "Angel Force, huh? I'm not surprised you're interested in them. I sensed trouble rolling off those guys the second they strolled in. They wanted to negotiate a deal on magic charges to blast the fish out of the sea. I can't stand that kind of fishing. Fishing is about finding your peaceful moments. Most of my guys, and a few of the girls, fish because it's their happy place. They relax and let their worries slide away. They don't always catch anything, but they go home with a sense of calm and a smile on their faces. You don't get that by dropping charges and waiting for things to go boom."

"That does seem unfair on the fish," I said. "Although I imagine no scaled beasty is a fan of fishy hunters. They'd rather stay in the water than have hooks stuck into their mouths and be yanked out for an unwanted photo opportunity with some smiling idiot."

He chortled and stroked a hand down his beard. "Yeah, some of the guys with points to prove love hooking those big fish and getting their photographs taken. We make a small fortune off them in summertime. We charge to take their pictures, and there's always a queue of red-faced guys with their catch of the day, wanting to capture that 'perfect' forever moment with their scaled prize."

"Have they already left?" Zandra asked. "We need to speak to them."

"They could be out on the water already. The tide is turning soon, so I told them to hurry if they wanted to get to the best fishing spots. They hired Blue Bertha. She's got navy paint and a picture of a kraken on the bow. She's beautiful and hard to miss. If she's still here, she sits just down the beach on the left."

"Thanks," I said, and we hurried out.

"There it is! They haven't gone yet." Zandra slowed and looked around. "I don't see any sign of Bael or Carlito. Let's take a look at the boat."

We rushed to the boat and peered inside. There was an ample supply of canned beer, snacks, and a big box of magic charges sitting in the bottom of the boat.

"Hey! That's my boat. Keep your hands off." Carlito strode over. Recognition lit his eyes, and he scowled. "You two again. You stalking me?"

"No, but we're hoping to solve Doyle's murder. Do you want to help with that?" I asked.

Carlito glowered at us as he dumped more supplies into the bottom of the boat. "I've got nothing to say. And I'm busy. I need to get out before the tide turns."

"Are you fishing alone?" Zandra asked. "Where's your friend?"

"Bael gets easily distracted by a pretty face," Carlito said. "He made other plans. His loss. I heard the fishing is great around here."

"Bael is entertaining a lady friend, and you're going sea fishing," I said. "You both seem remarkably composed, considering what happened to Doyle."

He shrugged. "Why shouldn't I go fishing? I'm under no threat. Doyle had a long line of enemies who wanted to chop his head off or blow him into tiny pieces and then laugh about it. We all knew this day was coming. I just never figured his long-lost kid would be the one to do it."

"Finn didn't do it," I said. "Which is why we're investigating other suspects."

Carlito stopped arranging his supplies in the boat. "And you're looking at me?"

"We're looking at everyone who had a close link with Doyle," Zandra said. "Do you mind telling us how long you've known each other?"

"Too long. Now, I'm going fishing. If you want to keep talking, you can come with me or get lost. I prefer the last option."

I looked at the water. It was calm, but I still didn't like the sea. As the bartender had said, you never knew what lurked in the murky depths.

Carlito climbed out of the boat and lifted his arms. The boat rose an inch off the pebbles, and he walked with it to the water's edge. "Last chance."

"We'll come with you," I said.

Zandra frowned. "Must we? I don't like boats."

"This won't take long. Once we're done, I'll translocate us to the shore, and we can investigate the seafood stand." I hopped into the boat, and Zandra clambered in after me.

Carlito smirked as he jumped in then used a blast of magic to get the boat out of the shallows, and we were soon zooming along, heading to deeper water.

Zandra pressed a hand against her stomach as her face turned green.

"Take deep breaths and keep your gaze fixed on the horizon," I murmured. "Your stomach will soon settle."

She gritted her teeth and nodded.

"You were telling us about how long you've known Doyle," I said to Carlito.

"Was I?" Carlito sat at the back of the boat as he steered.

"You need to take this seriously," I said. "Or don't you care what happened to your friend? Maybe you're glad he's dead."

"I already know what happened to him. He went off with Finn and got himself killed."

"But not by Finn's hand," I said.

"That's not what I've heard."

"You didn't approve of Doyle looking for his son?" I asked.

"I backed him. He was determined to do it, so I wished him well, but I couldn't figure out why he suddenly got so interested in finding Finn. Why dredge up the past?"

"Because he wanted to reconnect with his family?"

"Ha! Doubtful. Doyle was never exactly father of the year. I suppose you know about his rap sheet?"

Zandra nodded.

"This spot will do. It's supposed to be one of the best sites for nabbing wahoos or redfish." Carlito slowed the boat, and soon we were bobbing on the gentle waves. He tossed a magic charge into the water then grabbed a beer. "It'll be a few minutes before that activates. Then I'll have my first fish."

I peered into the water, aimed a murder mitten, and sank it below the chilly surface. I made contact and pulled out a large silvery fish.

Carlito's eyes widened. "Hey! No cheating."

"I didn't cheat. I'm a naturally skilled hunter. Ask Zandra. I bring her all kinds of delicious prey gifts."

"Yeah. I always welcome those gifts," Zandra said. She still looked green. "What kind of demon was Doyle?"

"Rage demon." Carlito glared at the fish as it flipped on my paw. "We all are. Anger makes us more powerful. You irritate someone or get them wound up about something, and it gives us a buzz."

I nodded as I inspected the fish I'd caught, whispered to it, and then gently cast it back into the water. "Finn's demon is similar."

"That's no surprise, given where he came from."

The water swelled beneath us, and the boat lifted as the charge took effect.

Carlito peered eagerly over the side of the boat and then frowned. "Where are they? I should have caught a few."

I looked away and suppressed a smile. I'd whispered a few words to the fish I'd caught, suggesting he took himself and his buddies far away from this boat. I was glad they'd listened and would live to swim another day without fear of having their brains blasted out by a lazy fisherman.

"I'll throw in another charge. They won't get away from me." Carlito tossed in more charges.

"Are you sure you don't know why Doyle suddenly decided to reunite with Finn?" I asked.

"He must have had his reasons. He was doing well with his business, so maybe he wanted to share the love. I don't know. Doyle was an impulsive guy. He could have gotten it into his head that he wanted bonding time with the son he'd abandoned." Carlito downed half a can of beer and then burped. "I'm glad I never had kids. Too much hard work. I never understand people's obsession with crotch goblins. All they are is an expense, and then they turn out ungrateful, hating you for supposedly ruining their lives. Not for me."

"I'm sure raising children has its challenges," I murmured.

"Hold on," Carlito said. "The fish will soon be floating."

The blast from the charges was so big it almost capsized the boat, and we were all left clinging to the sides.

No fish appeared.

"Have I got the right spot?" Carlito looked around and scowled. "I'm sure this was the place. Or was that salty old sea dog lying to me? Do people even fish out here? I don't see any other boats. If he's conned me, I'm getting my money back."

"What were you doing on the night Doyle died?" I asked.

Carlito remained standing, staring out at the horizon. "I was out with Bael. Then we crashed for the night."

"Weren't you staying at the same house as Doyle?"

He shook his head. "We have another place. Finn and Doyle decided they wanted a cozy night in, but we wanted some fun. We headed out, grabbed food and drinks, and hung around together for a while. Then we went back to our own place."

"What time did you get back to your rental?"

Carlito smirked. "Around midnight. We had a few more drinks then zonked out. The first we heard about what had happened was when that snooty angel got in contact." He shook his head. "We shouldn't have left them alone, but we had no idea the kid would burn up his own dad. I guess the rotten apple never falls far from the diseased tree."

"Diseased tree? That's what you thought of Doyle?" Zandra was still gripping the side of the boat and now breathing heavily.

"We hung out together and had fun, but Doyle was high maintenance. And since making all that money, he'd started acting like the big man, throwing his weight around. It got annoying. We were thinking about ditching him."

"Annoying enough to want him dead?" I asked.

Carlito pointed a finger at me. "You can't pin this murder on me. Finn was right in the middle of it. He's got guilt written all over him."

Perhaps he did, but the way Carlito talked about Doyle suggested there was no love lost between them. If he'd resented Doyle for his success, he may have grown bitter. It was a motive.

"What's the address of the rental you're staying at?" I asked.

"I never said it was a rental." Carlito fished out another can of beer.

"You're staying somewhere, right?" I asked. "A friend's house?"

"No, we don't know anyone in Crimson Cove."

"Where are you staying?"

He lifted one shoulder and focused on the water. "Where are those fish hiding?"

I stomped over and hit him with a stinging spell. "What's the problem? Why don't you want to tell us where you're staying?"

"Hey! No need for that." Carlito sighed as he rubbed his arm. "It's no big deal, but we may have borrowed a house without the owner's permission."

"You're squatting?" Zandra asked.

"Yeah, something like that. Ah! I see something below the water. It's my first catch." Carlito lunged forward, tipping the boat. It lurched from side to side, sending me sprawling.

I rolled over then rolled the other way as the boat kept tipping. "Stop jumping about or we'll capsize!"

"I can almost reach it. It's a huge fish!" Carlito kept leaning, and the boat kept tipping, and I kept rolling.

Zandra grabbed for me, but she wasn't fast enough, and suddenly, there was nothing beneath my paws as I plunged into the icy water.

Chapter 9

Fiery visitor

"I was very, very wet." I lay on my side as Sammy groomed me. He'd arrived twenty minutes ago to join us for breakfast at Vorana's, and I'd been updating him about the disastrous sea fishing attempt yesterday.

"You do taste a little like the sea." He paused from grooming my fur. "But you're still cute, even if you arc salty."

I sniffed one paw and grimaced. "Zandra fished me out of the waves in the nick of time. I was certain something with vicious fangs brushed against me when I was under the water. There are all kinds of sea creatures out there, just waiting for a tasty morsel like me to end up in the sea. Carlito was an idiot. He'd clearly never sea-fished before. The fact he was using magical charges proves he didn't know what he was doing."

Sammy flopped down next to me and sighed. "Do you think he's your killer?"

"He has a motive." I looked over my shoulder. "My lack of a tail is still an issue. I thought I'd gotten used to it, but yesterday's incident in the boat proves I need it back. I was wondering, and I never thought I'd say this, but maybe Tinkerbell could help. After all, she restored my fur to its now glorious, fluffy gleam."

"You should ask. She's been so happy since she formed a bond with Bilious. She's a different cat. I even heard her singing the other day. Tinkerbell never sings. If she can restore your tail, I'm certain she will."

"Her change has been remarkable."

"She's coming into animal control to check in with Barney," Sammy said. "And the trial is tomorrow, so she'll be around more. Once that's over, you could ask her."

I rolled over. "It's tomorrow! I've been so involved with what's going on with Finn that I lost track of time. Are you ready?"

Sammy nodded, seeming relaxed with his eyes half-closed. "We're taking Gaian and Lila down. With all of our testimonies and the evidence against them, they won't get away with what they tried to do to Crimson Cove."

"Or you," I said. "You and Tinkerbell were badly treated by them. So was Ember."

"And the angels have realized that. I won't be going inside, and my community service order has been approved. After the trial, I'll be a free cat, as long as I don't break the law." Sammy slid me a shy glance. "That means we can spend more time together."

"I look forward to it."

"Breakfast is ready!" Zandra yelled down the basement steps. "Are you two joining us?"

"We wouldn't miss it." I hopped off the bed and walked up the stairs with Sammy, a feeling of calm contentment inside me, so happy to have him with me again. "I'd like to be at the trial to support you."

He gently nudged me with his large head. "I'd like that, but you're too busy with this case. It's important you get Finn free and clear his name. You don't need me as a distraction."

"Maybe you are a distraction, but you're a wonderful one."

"Stay here and help Finn," Sammy said as we entered the kitchen. "You won't be able to see much of me, anyway. Witnesses are kept out of the way to avoid any tampering. But we can celebrate when I get back tomorrow. And I'll see if I can bring Tinkerbell with me."

"That sounds perfect," I said.

We settled into our seats around the kitchen table, and Vorana served kedgeree, minus the curry powder, for the felines and warm blueberry muffins for everyone else. The hatchling got a bowl of raw meat. Sage was in her usual seat, and the hatchling was in her chair with shaped arms so she couldn't flap her wings and destroy everyone's breakfast.

"I was just telling Vorana about our eventful trip yesterday," Zandra said.

"It confirmed my suspicions about boats. They're not to be trusted," I said.

"More like the moron who was steering the thing couldn't be trusted," Zandra said. "It's fortunate we didn't all end up in the sea. Carlito was flinging himself around trying to catch that fish, and he still failed to land so much as a barnacle."

I sniffed, recalling my plunge into the water. "I'm glad the fish got away. They deserve freedom, just like the rest of us."

"You may have taken a dunk, but at least you've got yourself a suspect," Vorana said.

"We need to convince Brodie to investigate Carlito," I said. "The way Brodie was talking yesterday, he seems convinced of Finn's guilt and that a confession was soon to be had."

Vorana thumped a hand on the table, her eyes blazing. "Finn didn't do this. I know there's evidence and an eyewitness, but I refuse to believe it. Someone's setting him up."

I nodded along, my mouth full of luscious kedgeree. I chewed and swallowed. "I was wondering if his memory got wiped by magic. He's got a specific blank spot at the most crucial time. He can't remember Doyle dying."

"Doesn't Brodie see that's a problem?" Vorana asked.

"He thinks Finn is playing a game," Zandra said. "Acting like he's lost his memory. But we found him, and he was in a mess. Maybe someone cast a spell over him and then whacked him on the head for good measure to ensure he didn't remember."

"What about this mysterious eyewitness?" Vorana reached over and cut Sage's breakfast into tiny chunks, so it was easier for her to eat. "What do we know about him?"

"Very little. And Brodie wasn't helpful in telling us who it was," I said.

"If I get my hands on this witness, I'll give him a shake and tell him to stop lying about Finn," Vorana said. "He's put our friend's freedom on the line. He must have been bribed or coerced. Maybe the real killer has something on him and is forcing him to lie."

"We're considering all possibilities," I said. "We'll keep digging until we find out who it is. And since we're in charge of the investigation to get Finn free, Angel Force can't withhold evidence from us. That would be unfair."

"I reckon Brodie would," Zandra grumbled. "The guy's already made up his mind about who's guilty."

"Then he's a foolish jerk, and I intend to tell him so when I see him," Vorana said. "Who wants more coffee?"

"We still have plenty of suspects to trawl through," I said. "We need to check Carlito's alibi, but there's also Bael, Doyle's other friend. He was busy entertaining a lady yesterday, so we didn't see him."

"And then there are the two women who came into the pizza parlor when we first met Doyle," Zandra said. "They need talking to."

I nodded. "They're all demons, so they have the power to incinerate. One of them must have been involved."

"Maybe they're working together." Sage hissed at the hatchling as she attempted to steal food from Sage's plate.

"We wondered about that too," I said. "Carlito said Doyle had recently come into a lot of money and was acting like he was something special. If his behavior didn't go down well with the group, they could have conspired to get rid of him."

"To take his money?" Vorana asked.

"Maybe to get rid of him and remove an irritation," I said. "We'll know more once we've interviewed them all."

Vorana shook her head. "I'll make up a basket of treats for Finn, and you can take it to him. Are you visiting him this morning before work?"

"We planned on dropping by," Zandra said. "I'm sure he'd appreciate some goodies to keep him occupied."

Vorana abandoned her breakfast, grabbed a wicker basket from the closet, and filled it with muffins, cookies, and other delicious treats to satisfy Finn's sweet tooth and give him something to smile about.

We finished our food, took the basket, said goodbye to everyone, and left the house with Sammy. Sammy headed to animal control for his daily check-in while we hurried to Angel Force to see Finn.

I stopped at the entrance to the open-plan office. Overnight, the place had been transformed. There was wedding paraphernalia everywhere. Boxes of fabric, flowers, and an enormous whiteboard littered with neatly written tasks relating to Cythera and Maverick's wedding was propped against one wall.

"We're back in wedding hell," Zandra muttered. "We should leave the basket and make a run for it. Finn will understand."

"He won't! And he'd appreciate a visit from us. We need to make sure he's being kept up to date."

"We could come back later, after work. All of this may be gone by then." She waved a hand at the gleaming white wedding mess.

"Perfect! Another opinion. It's exactly what we need." Maverick strode out of Cythera's office and over to us, grinning wildly. "Cythera has been so busy with Finn's investigation that we've barely had time to talk about the wedding, and it's so close. As you can see, there's still so much to do."

"Don't you have a wedding planner?" Zandra asked.

"We have three, and they're excellent, but I don't want them to overlook anything. I've written out all the tasks that still need doing and how we should oversee them. I was asking Cythera about last-minute changes to the seating plan, but she's too busy to talk. Maybe you can help."

Cythera stomped out of her office. "Murder over marriage! How many times do I have to tell you? Stop bothering other people. They care nothing about our wedding."

"We care very much about your wedding." I hopped onto a desk and inspected a sheet detailing the songs that would be sung at the ceremony. There were fifteen. "We're looking forward to the big day almost as much as you are."

Maverick pressed his hands together, his grin broadening. "It'll be the best day ever. And I don't want anything to go wrong."

Zandra gently cleared her throat. "I hate to be a downer about your special day, but things always go wrong at a wedding. There's no point in getting stressed. You need to roll with it."

Maverick's sunny expression dimmed. "We can't have anything go wrong."

"Zandra's right, you focus on the reason why you're marrying," I said. "You'll have this wonderful angel by your side for eternity so she can snap and snipe at you and tell you off for being too cheerful. Isn't that something to look forward to?"

Maverick stared at me for a second then roared with laughter. "There you go again, always making your little jokes about my dearest Cythera."

I looked at Cythera. She was glowering at all of us, her hands in fists.

"With all the work that's gone into making this day perfect, you'll have a ball," I said. "And we'll be there if you need any creases ironed out. Zandra has a lovely singing voice if you have time to fill at the ceremony. She's always singing in the shower."

"Maybe I should uninvite you," Cythera said.

"No! We must have them there, or I'll have to redo another seating plan." Maverick attempted to guide Cythera to a pile of papers detailing the seating information.

She jabbed a finger at the whiteboard. "You're interfering and causing problems. I've had all the wedding planners get in touch to say they don't know who they should take orders from."

"You. Definitely you," I said. "You give the best orders."

"Pipe down, fluffy," Cythera said.

I lifted a paw. "I'm here for useful suggestions and to make your life easier whenever you desire it."

"That's what we need, impartial advice," Maverick said. "I was talking to the higher angels for three hours last night about the flowers. They mean well, but their concept of our reality is sadly flawed."

"Are they still interfering?" Zandra asked.

"Alas, they think they're being helpful," Maverick said. "I haven't got the heart to tell them their ideas are a fraction on the side of impractical."

"I'd love to hear what they want you to do," I said.

"You're not going to," Cythera said. "What are you both doing here, anyway?"

"Visiting Finn," Zandra said. "We need to check he's doing okay, and Vorana made him a gift basket."

"I'll have to check that before it goes in to him." Cythera snatched the basket and inspected the contents. "I don't want you slipping in any magic or escape potions to assist him."

"As if we'd do such a thing," I said.

She shot me a glare. "I know you well enough to realize you'd do anything to save a friend."

"As would you if that friend was being accused of doing something he didn't do," I said.

"Finn is my employee." She shoved the basket back to Zandra.

"Cythera, I know you're under stress from the wedding, but you and Finn are friends, and I know you won't see him go down for a crime he didn't commit," I said.

"My love, the seating plan," Maverick pleaded. "If you can give me five minutes of your precious time, I must know if I've made the right changes. I don't want any bickering over dessert."

There was a crash in the reception area, and a few seconds later, Bael stomped in, demon energy sparking over him in jagged black and yellow flickers. His eyes were jet black, and a plume of ragged matt black feathers jutted out behind him. He growled when he saw us. "Where's that mutant? It's time he paid for killing my buddy."

Chapter 10

The truth is out

Maverick approached Bael, his hand out. "Calm down, my friend. There must be some mistake."

Bael thrust out a flaming fist, and Maverick flew back, hitting the floor with a grunt, a smear of black marring his pristine white shirt.

"Give me Finn. I know he did this. That runt killed Doyle, and I want revenge." Bael tipped back his head and roared, smoke billowing from his flared nostrils.

"You're getting nowhere near him." My hackles lifted, and I hopped onto Zandra's shoulder, connecting our magic. "Finn is being held for questioning, but no charges have yet been brought."

"And you'll never bring them. We all know you're best buddies with that murderer," Bael said. "He'll get away with this because he knows the right people."

"He won't if he's guilty. But you won't get away with what you've just done." Cythera helped

Maverick to his feet. "You can't walk in here and make demands. And you don't injure my fiancé."

Bael smirked and thrust out a blast of demon energy. It smashed into the enormous whiteboard, shattering it into pieces.

Maverick cried out in alarm and attempted to shield Cythera with his wings.

Cythera batted him aside with an exasperated sigh. "Angels, arrest the demon."

There were only three angels on duty, but they sprang into action and circled Bael, their wings flaring. The atmosphere crackled with tension as they faced off against the demon. Sparks of celestial and infernal energy danced in the air, illuminating the room with an eerie glow.

Bael's black wings flared as he summoned his demonic powers, his eyes glowing like hot coals. Across from him, the angels, their wings shimmering with an ethereal light, braced for the impending clash.

"Should we help?" Zandra whispered, magic primed in her hand.

"Let's see what the angels can do." I encouraged Zandra to inch out of the way of the fight. When demons fought, it was always messy.

Bael's lips curled into a wicked grin, revealing elongated, razor-sharp fangs. He unleashed a torrent of flames, a blazing inferno that roared toward the angels. The room became an arena of elemental forces, the fire hissing as it met the cool, protective magical barriers erected by the angels. The flames danced and writhed, a battle of heat and light.

One of the angels retaliated with a blast of radiant energy. Her hand extended, and from her palm, a beam of pure light shot forth, piercing the flames. The collision created a dazzling explosion that sent shockwaves through the room, knocking over furniture and shattering glass.

"They've been trained well," I murmured.

Zandra nodded. "They're holding their own."

I glanced over at Cythera, who Maverick was still attempting to protect. She looked calmly assured as her angels fought the troublemaker.

Another angel weaved intricate sigils in the air with swift movements of her hands. Her magic coalesced into a swirling vortex, forming a barrier that countered the searing heat. The swirls whipped around the flames, sending them spiraling back toward Bael in a twisted dance of fire and air.

Bael, his wings shrouded in dark shadows, summoned choking smoke that enveloped him, masking his movements. He launched toward the angels, his clawed hands slashing through the air. The clash of demonic and angel power created a shuddering boom that shook the office.

Bael's laughter echoed through the chaos as his form twisted. With a ferocious roar, he unleashed a barrage of projectiles. The angels weaved and dodged, their movements a dance of grace and precision as they deflected the attack.

A blast of flames shot into the open-plan office, and a second later, the dragon hatchling appeared! She was followed by Sammy, magic sparking all over his magnificent fur.

"Sorry! She sensed something bad was happening and came charging over here. I couldn't stop her," he said when he saw me, alarm in his eyes as he took in the devastation and glowering demon.

"Stop her before she burns the place down!" I yelled.

"Too late for that." Zandra stamped out a fire that had started in a recycling tray.

The hatchling stomped around, growling and puffing out smoke at anyone who got too close to her.

"Sammy!" I gestured at the baby. "Look after her. Pin her down if you must."

"I'm on it."

"Juno, get that hatchling out of here," Cythera commanded. "She's vulnerable."

"I'm trying. She thinks she's helping." I focused on coaxing the hatchling away from the scene of magical conflict, but she was too focused on Bael and his rage and refused to move.

"How would she have known anyone was in danger unless she had a bond with them?" Cythera's eyes widened, realization dawning. "Has this hatchling bonded with Finn? She's here to protect him?"

Bael's aggression erupted in a spell aimed at the hatchling and Sammy. Reacting swiftly, I channeled a surge of magic to knock Bael off his feet and then leaped onto his back, my murder mittens activated. He roared in anger, struggling so fiercely that I whipped around like I was on a fairground ride. One I wanted to get off.

Meanwhile, the hatchling danced around us, a mini creature of fire and fury, blasting flames toward Bael.

"Sammy, get her out of here. We don't want anyone getting hurt if she makes a mistake and shoots fire at the wrong person." I latched claws into Bael's feathers as he spun me again, attempting to knock me off his back.

Sammy's fur bristled as he tackled the hatchling to the floor, engaging in a grappling match as she squeaked her protests. He swiftly subdued her fiery outbursts and pinned her wings. The hatchling squawked and struggled, but she was going nowhere now she was under Sammy's masterful paws.

"Get her back home." As I issued instructions to Sammy, Bael's attempts to dislodge me continued. "Angels! A little help would be appreciated. I'm not doing this for your entertainment."

The wary angels responded swiftly, their celestial strength finally proving enough to restrain Bael's ferocity, now I assisted them, and with our combined efforts, we dragged him into an empty interview room.

Sammy's struggle with the hatchling persisted for a few more seconds before they vanished in a sparkle of magic, leaving behind a room marred by scorch marks, splintered furniture, and broken glass.

I released my hold on Bael and dropped to the floor, my breath ragged. Zandra was instantly by my side, concern etched across her features as she lifted me into her warm, welcoming embrace.

"Any injuries?" Her voice was a mixture of worry and relief.

"I'm not hurt," I assured her, my frustration mingling with the adrenaline coursing through me. "I am angry, though. How did the hatchling get here? Vorana should have been watching her more closely."

"We'll figure that out later," she whispered, her concerned gaze still focused on me.

"With me, you two." Cythera's voice came from the doorway. She gestured for us to follow her out of the room, then turned and stomped away, her large wings fluttering and hands fisted.

I was almost more fearful of her than the cussing demon being restrained in the interview room.

Zandra closed the door, and we faced Cythera's intense scrutiny.

"Explain yourselves." She crossed her arms in an unyielding stance and fixed us with an icy stare.

"There's nothing to explain," I said as levelly as possible. "You saw what happened. We saved this building from being incinerated by an angry demon. And where's a warrior angel when you need one? I thought Brodie was leading on this case."

"He's out gathering evidence." Cythera's gaze didn't waver. "How did that hatchling know Finn and you were in trouble?"

"It must have been a coincidence. Perhaps she was walking by and smelled smoke. She likes smoke." I attempted to deflect her probing. "Don't focus on that. We have a suspect to interrogate. Bael came here to kill Finn!"

"Don't mess with me." Cythera's words were sharp. "That hatchling would have no idea what was going on here unless she has a bond with one or both of you. Which is it?"

"You know a lot about baby dragons. Did you study them during your training?" I asked.

"You're hiding things from me." Cythera's frustration at our concealment was as evident as the two red dots of color on her cheeks. "The moment I saw that creature in Vorana's kitchen, I should have contacted the dragons and had it picked up. The story about her temporarily fostering the creature isn't true, is it?"

"We didn't lie about Vorana looking after the hatchling until a permanent home is found for her," I stated truthfully.

Zandra nodded along with me. "The dragon won't be living with Vorana for much longer."

"I don't believe you," Cythera said. "And I will get to the truth, eventually."

My outward demeanor remained composed, but my thoughts raced. Cythera's determination could unravel our carefully constructed story about the hatchling. We were running out of time to find a solution for our small dragon companion.

"Let's deal with the most important thing. We have a fuming demon to interrogate," I said.

Cythera's scowl revealed her inner anger dialog was barely under control. "Don't think I'm letting the dragon issue slide." She yanked open the door and strode to the interview room. We followed, the weight of the situation pressing heavily upon me.

Zandra pressed her hand against my side, a sign she knew we'd just added an extra complication to our lives.

"Will you behave yourself, or do I need to keep my angels guarding you?" Cythera asked Bael.

"I don't need no stinking guard," he retorted. "But I will see Finn. He's gotta pay for what he's done."

"And if he's guilty, he'll do so," Cythera said. "But you don't have the right to demand justice." She glared at Bael until he looked away.

"So long as you do your job properly, I won't be a problem," Bael said.

"Are you sure? Or shall I put you in shackles so you can barely move while we question you?"

"Question me? About what?" Bael's confusion was clear as he glared up at her from his seat.

"About what you were doing at the time of Doyle's murder," I said.

"You've got to be kidding me. You want to pin this on me?" Bael shook his head. "Carlito said you've been snooping around and asking questions that were none of your business."

"We've been investigating a murder," I said. "We need to ensure the guilty party is found."

"You already have the guilty party. He was at the crime scene with blood all over his hands. And I know there's an eyewitness."

"Let's take this back a few steps," Cythera said, and we all took a moment to settle into seats. "Angels, you're dismissed. But stay close in case Bael misbehaves again."

"You make me sound like a child," he grumbled.

"Your behavior suggests you have little control over your abilities, so I must treat you with the appropriate amount of discipline," Cythera said.

I settled on the table and glared at Bael. He could have harmed Sammy and the hatchling when he'd been blasting out his demon power, and that was unforgiveable. "Your aim was way off when you fought. What was the point of hitting the wedding whiteboard?"

"Better that than someone's head." Bael smirked. "I was making a point. Showing you I shouldn't be messed with."

"The whiteboard will never come at you again," I said. "You showed it who's the boss. Perhaps some of that rogue demon energy accidentally hit Doyle. You covered up your mistake by framing Finn."

Bael bared his teeth. "I can tell you right now, I had nothing to do with what happened to Doyle."

"Yet you know a lot about the crime scene," I said. "Why would that be if you weren't there?"

"People talk. This murder is all everyone's talking about. And I've been discussing things with Carlito."

"What did you talk about?" Cythera asked.

Bael shuffled around in his seat then linked his hands behind his head and leaned back. "We both thought Doyle reuniting with Finn was a bad idea, but we backed him anyway. We figured Doyle must be getting bored and needed a challenge. And what's more challenging than reuniting with some kid you ditched because you didn't think he was good enough for you?"

"That's the reason Doyle abandoned Finn?" I asked. "He told you that?"

"He didn't have to. Everyone knows how rough life is raising a kid who's a half-angel, half-demon in our community. Not worth it. It was the best he could do, give up the kid and get on with his life," Bael said.

"Doyle told us he gave up Finn because he was having personal problems," Zandra said.

Bael shrugged. "I couldn't comment on that."

"How long have you known Doyle?" Cythera asked.

"We've been kicking around with each other since we were teenagers. A long time."

"You were around when he was in a relationship with Finn's mother?" I asked.

"A relationship! It was barely that. They were a pair of rebellious idiots who thought it would outrage people when they were hanging out together. I doubt they even liked each other that much."

"They must have liked each other enough to produce Finn," I pointed out.

"You drink enough and anyone seems attractive," Bael said. "Even an angel. Doyle wasn't ready for responsibility, and he didn't want the hassle that came with having a hybrid kid. Especially not an angel-demon hybrid. He should have stayed away from Finn, especially when he found out he worked for Angel Force. The humiliation."

"Finn is an excellent employee," Cythera said. "He's an asset to the force."

"Which is exactly my point, blondie. Finn is more angel than demon. That's hardly something you want to show off at a family party. But Doyle wasn't for turning. He was a stubborn son of a gun, and once he made his mind up about something, he went through with it even if he could see the results would be disastrous. And what a disaster this turned out to be."

"Why do you think Finn killed Doyle?" I asked.

"Because of their fight," Bael replied.

"Tell us about the fight," Cythera said. "When did it happen?"

"It was earlier that evening, the night Finn killed Doyle."

"Allegedly," I muttered.

"Yeah, whatever. We'd all eaten and had a few drinks, when Finn started grilling Doyle about why he abandoned him, and what gave him the right to give up his own child. Doyle laughed it off and told Finn several times that they'd talk in private when they didn't have company, but the dumb kid dug his heels in. I guess they're more alike than I realized. It got intense."

"Where was this?" I asked.

"At Doyle's rental. We went back with them for a drink, and it kicked off. Carlito and I headed out to find some fun, rather than watch those two go at it."

"You were with Carlito the whole evening?" Cythera asked.

"Sure. We went out, had more drinks, more food, hung around the town for a while, then we went back to our place."

"The home you're squatting in?" I asked.

Bael snorted. "Squatting! I'm not some homeless bum begging for change. I don't need to squat. I've got cash, but I like to keep it for fun stuff, not rent."

"Carlito has told us you're staying in a place without the owner's permission," I said.

"Oh, did he?" He blew out a breath. "That guy talks too much."

"Why find somewhere else to stay rather than stay in the rental with Doyle?" I asked.

"It was Doyle's idea. He figured things could get intense between him and Finn. He said if the kid had the same attitude as him, sparks would fly, so we should find an alternative crash pad. The problem was, he sprung this genius idea on us once we got to Crimson Cove, so we had to improvise, and I couldn't be bothered dragging around town looking for a hotel."

"Where exactly is the place you're staying in?" Cythera asked.

Bael's bottom lip jutted out. "You don't need to go there."

"We do," Zandra said. "How do we know you're telling the truth? You could have been staying with Doyle when you decided to kill him and frame Finn."

"Hey! I wouldn't do that." He smirked. "Although it's not a bad idea. Doyle had issues. I mean, I liked the guy, but he's been so full of himself recently. And he said he'd pay for this entire trip, but then kicked us out of the accommodation, left us stranded, and expected us to figure things out on our own."

"That must have been frustrating," Cythera said, not a trace of sympathy in her tone.

"We found a solution. Real nice digs, too. Posh."

"Give us the address," Cythera said. "We need to confirm if you're telling the truth."

Bael sighed. "What's the point? We haven't messed up the place. The owner will get it back in almost pristine condition, minus the food in the fridge and a few bottles of booze. Well, a few dozen bottles of booze."

"What did you do with the owner?" I asked.

He grinned. "He's been looked after."

"Have you hurt him?" Cythera asked.

"No! I'm not a monster. He's safely locked in his own wine cellar. I expect by now, he'll be drunk and happy."

Cythera's wings extended slowly. "You restrained someone so you could squat in their home?"

"Better that than kill him."

"Give us the details," I demanded.

Bael grumbled as he scribbled some information on a piece of paper Cythera gave him.

She opened the door and summoned an angel. "Process Bael and take him to a cell. Make sure he's nowhere near Finn."

"You can't lock me up!" Bael protested. "I've done nothing wrong. I've been helpful. I answered your stupid questions, and I didn't burn this place down when you wouldn't let me teach Finn a lesson."

"You fought in my office, injured my fiancé, and smashed my precious wedding whiteboard. You'll pay for those crimes." Cythera stepped back as an angel came in and took Bael to the cells.

"We need to get to that house," I said. "Make sure the owner really is okay."

Zandra nodded as she stood from her chair. "Give me two minutes to grab a coffee then we'll leave."

I was about to hop off the table when Cythera grabbed me rudely by the scruff. "Not yet, we don't. We need to clear up this dragon mess."

Chapter 11

Scruffed!

Cythera dumped me on her desk and slammed the office door in Zandra's face as she hurried over from the kitchen.

I shook out my glorious fur and glowered at her. "You're fortunate we're on friendly terms. Few people can scruff me and get away with it. And what's Zandra done that warrants such rudeness?"

Zandra shoved open the door. "Hey! What's going on?"

"Get in here, too. You're both involved. Whenever Juno is up to mischief, you always cover for her." Cythera yanked Zandra into the room and slammed the door shut again.

"Not always." Zandra rubbed the top of her arm. "Juno can be sassy at times, but you must be used to it by now."

"Her sass I can tolerate, but not her lies," Cythera said.

"I cloud some truths, but it's always for your benefit. And when you need to know the things we conceal from you, you will," I said.

"Unacceptable. Tell me everything about the dragon hatchling." Cythera flared her wings, blocking our escape. "Leave nothing out, or no one gets out of this room."

"Not even for a comfort break or snacks?" I asked.

She growled at me.

"There's little we can tell you," I said on a sigh. "She's adorable, though, don't you think? And a white dragon, so rare."

"I care nothing for her color or how adorable she looks. What bothers me is that she knew you. She came to your defense when you were in trouble."

"It looked like that, but it was chance she was here," I said.

"I don't believe you."

"Don't worry about a dragon. You've already got enough to worry about," Zandra said. "Did you see what happened to your wedding whiteboard? Destroyed. Smashed into a thousand pieces."

Cythera waved away the comment. "I'm sure Maverick has a backup plan. He's almost as organized as me. I must know about this hatchling. It's not safe to have one in Crimson Cove unattended."

"She was with Sammy," I said. "My marvelous snuggle buddy had everything under control."

"The devastation in the office suggests otherwise."

"That was mainly the demon's fault," Zandra said. "Bael really had a terrible aim. He should get his eyesight checked."

"The infant also had a terrible aim, incinerating anything that moved. Why do that if it had no connection to either of you?" Cythera asked. "When a hatchling bonds with someone, they protect them."

I exchanged a worried look with Zandra. If we told Cythera the truth, she'd be furious.

Cythera pursed her lips. "You're not leaving this office until I know everything."

"Oh, look! There's Maverick! You should see how your fiancé is doing," I said. "He was heroic, coming to your defense when Bael stormed in. That's a sign of excellent character."

"Maverick is fine. He's picking through what's left of the wedding paraphernalia he insisted on bringing here." She tapped her foot on the floor. "Tell me what's going on."

"It's not our tale to tell," I said with some reluctance. "And if we reveal the whole story, we'd be breaking a confidence."

Cythera tipped back her head. "This has to do with Finn, doesn't it?"

We remained silent.

She glared at both of us in turn. "He's been absent-minded, showing up late for shifts, frequently looks charred around the edges, and his current cologne has the distinct undertone of smoke."

"How perceptive of you," I said. "Maybe he's trying a new look. Gothic Smoke. Is that a thing? If it isn't, it should be."

"Finn was the reason the dragon hatchling barged in. She has a connection to him, not you."

We still remained silent.

"I can ask him myself," Cythera said. "And I can keep asking him until he gives in. I don't want to stress him given his current problems, but don't think I won't press this issue until I get everything out in the open so I know how to deal with it."

"Perhaps you should talk to him," Zandra said after an awkward silence had enveloped us.

"I'm sure he doesn't want to be hassled. He's got enough to think about," I said.

Maverick burst into the office. "My love, there's not much I've been able to save, but the song sheets are unharmed."

"I care nothing about the songs at our wedding," Cythera snapped.

Hurt flickered in Maverick's eyes. "But you do care, don't you? We've worked so hard to make everything perfect. The whiteboard has been destroyed. I have notes, but it'll take me hours to put everything back together. I can do it with your help."

"Don't bother. We'll improvise," Cythera said.

I dropped my jaw. Cythera never improvised with anything. Her life was a series of plans, to-do lists, and reports that needed to be signed off.

Maverick hesitated in the doorway, his hands clasped together. "I... Of course. I see you're busy.

I'll leave. I don't want to get in the way." He turned away and eased the door closed.

"Cythera! Badly handled. Maverick is excited about your special day. Go after him and make amends," I said.

"He'll have to get used to being talked to that way once we're married," Cythera said.

"Then you're due for a miserable marriage," Zandra said. "The guy is being nice and trying to help. The lack of interest you've shown in your wedding suggests you still don't want to go through with it. Is that true?"

Her nostrils flared. "I never said that. And we're not discussing my wedding."

"We should. Maverick's kind. He puts up with your cold shoulder and clipped words all the time, so give him some slack," I said. "Don't push him away, or you'll end up in a chilly bed with a stone for a heart."

She huffed out a breath before pulling open the office door. "Maverick! Return to me."

He dashed back. "Yes, my love?"

Cythera glanced our way then focused on Maverick. "I'd... I'd appreciate it if you could go to the bakery and see how Tia's doing with our cake. At least we'll have that on our special day."

His face instantly brightened. "That's an excellent idea. I'll report back as soon as possible. Would you like me to bring you—"

She shut the door on him and turned to us. "Happy now?"

"It's a small positive step," I said, "but you need to go to New Bride School and learn a few tricks of the trade."

Cythera grumbled under her breath then sighed. "I'm aware we have things to work on, but right now, this investigation takes precedence. Maverick understands that. I won't let one of my angels go down for a crime he didn't commit. And if it turns out he did it, then..."

"Then what?" I asked.

"Then I have a problem I don't know how to solve. The fact Finn's keeping secrets from me is making things more difficult. How can I trust him? If he lied about the hatchling, maybe he lied about being innocent of murder." Her blue eyes shone with tears for a second before her stern exterior snapped back into place.

"You should talk to Finn," Zandra said. "Straighten things out with him."

"I will. Follow me." Cythera marched out of the office.

I hopped onto Zandra's shoulder as we hurried behind her. "Finn's been keeping this secret for too long. It's time more people got involved."

"What if Cythera goes to the dragons, though?" Zandra whispered. "Finn will end up toasted. The kind of toast that gets stuck in the toaster and sets off the smoke alarm when it turns to ash."

"Even though Cythera always looks like she keeps things on the straight and narrow, she'll bend to keep Finn safe. There was almost a flicker of affection on her face when she talked about proving him innocent."

"Stop whispering behind my back." Cythera opened the door to the main cells. "And I'd strongly advise you to encourage Finn to tell the truth when I confront him."

I hissed at her, my patience with this frustratingly grumpy angel growing thin. "And I suggest you stop barking orders at us like we're your employees. We're here to help, not to be snapped at."

Zandra pressed her lips together, her eyes wide.

We walked the rest of the way in a curt silence until we got to Finn's cell.

"Is everything okay?" He was on his feet the second he saw us. "I can smell smoke."

"Bael dropped by," I said. "He accused you of murdering Doyle and said he wanted payback."

"He attacked the team?" Alarm crossed Finn's face. "Did anyone get hurt?"

"Only Bael. Thanks to some help from a small friend of ours," I said.

Finn cocked his head, his expression curious. "A small friend?"

"Tell me about your infant dragon," Cythera said.

Finn gulped. "What dragon?"

"The time for deception is over. An angry infant dragon roared into the office and attacked Bael. Between them, they devastated the place. If it weren't for Sammy's swift intervention, we may have lost the entire building."

"Sammy was here too?" Finn asked. "I've missed a lot."

Cythera's expression tightened. "The dragon was here because she has a connection to you. I don't know how you achieved it, but that hatchling came to protect you."

"It's illegal for any other magical being to look after a dragon hatchling. The dragons always care for their infants. Everyone knows that." Finn glanced at us. "I mean, if someone brought one to the sanctuary in need of care, I wouldn't turn it away because that would be cruel, but that's all I'd do."

"The infant looked healthy to me. Even a little on the podgy side."

I thumped her with a murder mitten. "Hey! That's baby fat. She'll grow into her chub."

Cythera shook her head at Finn. "You show up stinking of smoke and bleary-eyed most days because you're looking after a hatchling. What possessed you to keep her?"

Finn was silent for a long time, his gaze on the floor. "I... I don't know who it was, but someone left a dragon egg outside the sanctuary. I meant to return it, but I've been so busy, and the egg was dormant. But one day, she sang to me, and we bonded. I haven't been able to let her go."

Cythera's wings flared. "You absolute, total, cretinous moron. That's a death sentence. When the dragons find out, they'll come for her and you, and there'll be little I can do to stop them."

"They may already have an idea something is amiss," I said. "We've seen a dragon or two lurking about."

Cythera gave a most uncharacteristic squeak. "We've already had dragons in the area and I don't know about it?"

"They've been scouting around," Zandra said. "Nothing definite, but we recognize the signs."

"And a dragon most likely burned down the barn at my sanctuary as a warning," Finn said. "They know the hatchling is here."

"Then give her back!"

Finn winced at Cythera's shrill tone. "How do you give up something you have such a strong bond with?"

"You give her up or you die," Cythera said. "Do you want to die?"

"It's not that simple," I said. "I'd be unable to give up Zandra, no matter the problem it created. It's a shame you don't have a bonded familiar because then you'd understand Finn's dilemma."

"I'm grateful I don't feel a connection to anyone."

"Except Maverick, your almost husband." I twitched my whiskers. "Or have you forgotten he's currently investigating your wedding cake under the strictest of orders from his beloved?"

"Of course not! I didn't mean him. Although dealing with an overly attentive fiancé is more than enough to handle," Cythera said. "Add an irritating fluffy or something with scales, and it would be too much to handle."

"I have help!" Finn said. "The hatchling is fond of Juno, and Vorana and Sage look after her when I'm here. I can make things work once I've ironed out the creases."

"She must be returned to the dragons," Cythera said. "Crimson Cove is at risk every second she remains here. What if the dragons discover she's here and that you've been conspiring with others to conceal her from them? They could devastate the town as revenge."

Finn hung his head. "I can't let her go."

"You're being selfish," Cythera said. "And irresponsible."

"It's not his fault," I said. "He's under a dragon thrall, so he has little control over his desire to keep her. And the baby picked him because he's an excellent parent."

"He's a thoughtless idiot, and he's bringing trouble our way."

"I know! Everything you're saying makes sense, but the second I see that hatchling, I forget all about it," Finn said. "I only feel love."

"And she's another reason why Finn would never kill Doyle. Why kill his father and risk losing the baby he so clearly adores?" I asked.

"She's not his baby. We don't need an out-of-control dragon to deal with. Fix this or I will." Cythera turned and stomped to the end of the corridor.

"How can I fix anything while I'm stuck in here?" Finn watched her go.

"Think about what you've done, while I figure out what to do with you," Cythera said. "You two, with me."

"We'll do our best to calm her down," Zandra said.

"How did she even find out?" Finn asked. "Did you tell her?"

I shook my head. "Cythera was figuring it out for herself, and then the hatchling burst in to defend you when Bael threw his weight around and demanded justice, and the game was up."

He sighed. "If I get out of this murder charge, I'll have to face Cythera's anger. I'm not sure which one is worse."

"Juno! Zandra! With me, now."

"You'd better go," Finn said. "Don't give her any more reasons to be mad."

We dashed out of the cells and hurried after Cythera, who was striding toward the main door.

"Where are we going?" I asked. "Not to see a dragon, I hope."

"To confirm Carlito and Bael's alibis. I need something concrete to focus on."

"What about Finn and his hatchling problem?"

"I need time to consider his punishment and what to do now I have this information." She glanced at us as we stopped outside. "Do you remember the address?"

"I think so," Zandra said. "Don't be too hard on Finn. He's doing his best."

"His best is a pustulated unicorn horn explosion with a side order of rancid vampire dirt. I'll meet you there. Don't delay." Cythera took to the wing and vanished.

"She's still being barky with her orders," I said. "If it weren't for Finn needing our help, I'd suggest we abandon this case."

Zandra strolled along. "I'll let you remind her not to bark at us."

"I'm worried about Finn," I said. "He shouldn't have concealed the hatchling from Cythera."

"We know why he did it, though. She'd have sent his baby back to the dragons and probably fired him."

I twitched my whiskers. "She'd be a fool to let him go."

"Before we focus on the issue of the hatchling, we need to get him off this murder charge."

I hopped onto her shoulder. "I'll cast a translocation spell."

We arrived as Cythera touched down. She barely spared us a glance as she marched toward a house.

"We're in the posh part of town." Zandra looked up at a creamy beige stone detached house. A grand entrance with ornate double doors made of rich mahogany wood welcomed guests. The place was in darkness.

"It looks like nobody's home," I said.

Zandra peered up at the windows. "They've probably abandoned the place and found another unsuspecting victim to exploit."

"Bael said they took the owner to the wine cellar," Cythera said. "There should be an outside hatch that takes us down there without having to break in."

It took a few minutes of poking around, but we discovered a set of double doors that held promise. Unfortunately, they were locked with steel chains and a sizeable padlock. I called Cythera over, and she took a moment to look at the chains. She rested her hands over them and blasted out magic, leaving behind nothing but sparkles.

"Handy trick," I said.

"I want this case solved. No more delays." She pulled open the hatch door, peered into the gloom, and marched down the stone steps.

We hurried after her. It took a few seconds to find the lights, but when they flicked on, they revealed a man lying on his side with a red stain on his shirt.

Chapter 12

Another body?

Cythera rushed to the man's side and leaned over him. "He's still breathing."

"Alcohol fumes, judging by the smell in this place." I wrinkled my booping snooter as I took in the rows upon rows of booze. "Why does one person need so many bottles of wine?"

"Don't gawk. Come and help," Cythera said.

Zandra walked over and peered down at the man. She rolled her eyes. "That's not blood on his shirt. It's probably expensive claret."

"He has a strong pulse," Cythera said. "And I see no injuries on his body. He does smell like a fermented grape."

The man groaned, and his eyes flickered open. "An angel. So pretty." He reached up to touch Cythera's face, but she swatted away his hand.

"What's your name?" she asked.

"You can call me Daddy. Who are you, beautiful?"

Cythera stepped back out of his reach. "You're drunk."

"But you're still beautiful." His gaze slid to us. "And you are?"

"Greetings! We're your rescuers," I said, "although it appears you've been content to be trapped in your own wine cellar. What's your real name, Daddy?"

He attempted to stand, but fell back and hit his head on the stone floor. He grunted. "Shamus Silver."

Cythera sighed, held out a hand, and yanked him to his feet. He stumbled into her. "Shall we dance?"

"Control yourself. We need to know how you got down here."

He looked confused. "There are steps. You walk up and down them."

Cythera sighed, while I held in a laugh. "Did you come down here voluntarily?"

"Oh, no. You mean the two demons who broke into my home?"

"Yes! Tell us more about them," Cythera asked.

"Shall we dance first?"

"You'll be under arrest for assault if you lay another finger on me." Cythera's wings flared.

Shamus chuckled. "Calm yourself, pretty. I'm just having a giggle with you. I was having a quiet night in alone—I'm not married, in case you're interested—and there was this thudding on the front door. I ignored it, since I wasn't expecting anyone." He looked around. "I'm sure there was a bottle of wine here somewhere."

"It's on your shirt," I said. "Those stains will never come out."

He looked down at his shirt and laughed. "Oh, yeah. I tripped just after I opened a bottle. Such a waste. It was a 1964 Merlot. Full-bodied, just like this hottie."

"Focus on the demons," Cythera hissed at him. "How did they get in?"

"I let them in. Well, I opened the door to see what the noise was about. They barged in and said they'd come to stay. Before I fought back, one of them knocked me out, and they must have dragged me down here." He touched a small egg-sized lump on the side of his head.

"Did you try to get out or call for help?" Cythera asked.

"I tried. But my gadgets are upstairs. I'm a tech mage, you see, so I need my gizmos to activate my magic. I'm almost powerless without them. I mean, I can do a few party tricks, but ask me to go up against two angry demons and I'll put my hands up and wave the white flag of surrender. I'm not a coward, but I'm also not an idiot." Shamus winked at Cythera. "Other than the whack on the head, they haven't been mean to me. They even brought down food and a corkscrew so I could keep myself occupied."

"I see you've had quite a prisoner party." There were takeout cartons and empty wine bottles scattered around.

"Nothing else to do, so why worry? They said they only wanted the place for a few days and then they'd let me out."

"They're suspects in a murder investigation," I said.

His eyes widened. "Who did they kill?"

"Another demon. How long have they been staying here?"

"A few days? Maybe two nights. Definitely more than one night." Shamus thought about it for a few seconds. "Yeah, pretty certain they were here for a couple of nights. They brought me back a cold burger and fries and a pizza on another night, so I've had two dinners while I've been down here."

"Are you certain?" Cythera's gaze went to the numerous empty wine bottles on the floor.

"Not a hundred percent, but they were always noisy when they came in. They'd put on loud music and bang around. I reckon they were here those nights. Did they really off someone?"

"We're looking into it," Cythera said. "Let's get you out of here. You may need medical attention for your head injury."

"I'm good, unless you want to kiss me better." Shamus stepped back and almost fell as Cythera glowered at him. "I do have a headache. I don't want to see a doctor, though. I've got healing magic upstairs."

"You're most likely dehydrated," I said.

"Yeah, maybe. I need a coffee, a spell, and my own bed. Sleeping down here isn't fun. Want to join me?" He grinned at Cythera.

Cythera made a noise of disgust in the back of her throat. "You two, deal with him. Sober him up."

"Anyone would think we work for her," Zandra muttered as Cythera marched back up the stone steps.

"I love a bossy woman," Shamus said.

"Don't love that one. She's about to be married," Zandra said.

"Oh! Wait! That's Cythera. Of course, I knew I recognized her. Everyone's talking about her marriage. Well, she's definitely off-limits. Shame. She's cute."

"Let's go get you some strong coffee and see if there's any common sense lying around," I said.

Twenty minutes later, after we'd gotten Shamus up the steps and into the main house, we left him with his coffee and complaints about the mess Bael and Carlito had left behind.

"I'm unhappy with Shamus's statement," Cythera said as we joined her outside. "If he spent the whole time getting drunk, he's not reliable."

"Which is good," I said. "It means Carlito and Bael remain on the suspect list."

"How about we talk to the neighbors?" Zandra pointed at a curtain twitching in the house next door.

The curtain stopped moving as we approached. Before we knocked, a small, rotund man with brilliant green eyes and an enormous fake fur collar opened the door. He wore a red velvet robe with an emblem of a mushroom on the breast pocket.

"We're investigating a disturbance at your neighbor's house," Cythera said by way of introduction. "Shamus Silver?"

"Yes, I know Shamus." The man stroked the fur collar with a plump hand.

"And you are?"

"Roland Moldsworth. I'm president and founder of the Fungal Remedies Apothecary School. We're opening a branch in Crimson Cove next month." He patted the mushroom emblem on his robe.

"Do I know about this?" Cythera looked at us as if she expected an answer.

"I've heard of the mushroom apothecary groups," I said. "You do wonderful work with underprivileged communities, giving out free medicine when magic isn't available."

"We do!" He beamed with pride. "But there aren't enough of us to go around, which is why we need a new school to train the next generation of magic using mycologists. Fungus can oddly repulse people, even though it's fascinating. Did you know—"

"We don't have time to chat," Cythera said. "We have an active investigation to deal with."

"Oh! I know you." Roland's eyes widened. "You run Angel Force. And you're about to marry. I received the beautiful note about the cake everyone is getting. So thoughtful."

"I'm glad." Cythera glanced at us. "These are my... assistants. Have you noticed anything strange going on at the house next door?"

"Of course! I contacted Angel Force about it. I sent in a complaint about the noise."

"What sort of noise did you hear?" I asked.

"Bangs and explosions. It sounded like there was a party in the backyard a few nights ago. Well, every night, actually. What's going on? Is Shamus okay?"

"He'll be fine once his hangover clears," Cythera said. "Did you notice anyone visiting him?"

Roland nodded. "Two men. Big and brawny. I don't like to judge solely on appearance, but they looked like trouble. And ever since they arrived, I've barely been able to sleep because of the noise. I thought about knocking on the door and asking them to keep it down, but I didn't think they'd listen to me."

"How often did you see them?" I asked.

"Every day they were staying here. They'd leave by noon, most likely to get food, then stay out late. When they came back, they appeared drunk. That was their routine since they arrived."

"What about two nights ago?"

"The same. Although they were barely standing that night. They were holding each other up and carrying bottles. Disgraceful behavior. Once they were inside, they didn't leave."

I jerked back in surprise when the fur collar around his neck moved. A pair of big, black eyes peered at me and growled.

"Be nice, Nimbus," Roland said. "These are our new friends. We must welcome them."

"What is that?" I was intrigued by the curious creature draped around him. I could see no legs or tail, just a mass of fur and glinting eyes.

"Nimbus is special," Roland said. "He's my companion animal."

The fluffy snake-like creature kept glaring at me and softly growling.

"When was the last time you saw the two individuals who caused all the noise?" Cythera asked.

Roland squinted. "Not today. Maybe yesterday? Yes, let me check." He bustled away from the door and returned with a small notebook in his hand, which he flicked through. "The last time one of them showed up was yesterday afternoon, just before four o'clock. He left an hour later, and I haven't seen them since."

"You keep note of your new neighbors' movements?" I asked.

"Of course. You never know when trouble may come calling. Is that what happened here?"

"There's been a suspicious death," Cythera said.

"At Shamus's house? It's not him, is it? He's an absolute lush, but I don't wish him harm."

Nimbus reacted to Roland's alarm by undulating around his neck, his fur flaring.

"There was no death at Shamus's house," Cythera said swiftly, "but not far from here. It was a friend of the demons who've been staying here."

"Demons! I knew it. I could tell just by looking at them. Oh dear, Nimbus, what should we do? It's not safe here. I shouldn't have bought this house on impulse, but it was such a good deal."

"It's very safe in Crimson Cove," Cythera reassured him. "There's no need to panic."

"Panic, we must!" Nimbus said, his voice a croaky rasp. He grew even larger as he curled himself around Roland's middle. "Danger. We flee."

"Yes! I could stay with my sister. Although you don't get along with her teacup pig, do you? I'm sure we'll manage in the short term." Roland's hands trembled, and he almost dropped his notepad.

"There's no need to go anywhere," Cythera said. "We're just checking suspects' movements to rule them out of the investigation."

"What if you can't rule them out? They looked like untrustworthy types. I'd never seen them before, and I monitor all of Shamus's visitors."

"Shamus must appreciate having such an attentive neighbor," I said.

"He hates it. He called me a nosy busybody and told me to get a life, but how can I have a life if I'm not safe in my own home?" Roland pressed a hand to his companion animal. "Nimbus, collect your favorite toys. We can leave in under an hour."

"Leave now," Nimbus said. "Not safe. Murder!"

"You should reassure your companion, not alarm him," I said to Nimbus.

"Protect him, I do," Nimbus grumbled. "Can barely look after himself."

"My sister will know what to do. She doesn't like me living alone," Roland said. "We'll pack our bags and go."

"It's your choice." Cythera spoke through gritted teeth. "Is there anything else you can tell us about the demons you saw?"

Roland was already pulling down coats from a nearby peg and looking at the pile of shoes by the door. "Once they were inside the house, I didn't see them again. I just heard the noise. Should I take my waterproof? And we mustn't forget your fur iron, Nimbus. He hates getting too fluffy. Oh, there's so much to think about."

"Thanks for your time," Zandra said. "We'll leave you to your packing."

We left Roland and Nimbus worrying about shoes and coats and headed back toward town.

"His testimony is reliable," Cythera said after a moment of silence. "It means Carlito and Bael are in the clear."

"But we all agree Finn isn't the killer," I said.

"I'll defend him for as long as I can," Cythera said. "But the evidence against him is mounting."

"Then we find new evidence that proves his innocence."

Cythera's gaze lowered. "We'll keep looking."

I didn't like the defeated tone in her voice, but there was no way we were giving up on Finn. He was innocent. We just needed to prove it.

Chapter 13

Damning evidence

Cythera was slumped in the seat behind her desk, her tired gaze flitting around her office. "This confirms it. Roland put in a noise complaint on the night of the murder. He described seeing two drunken rough types entering the house Carlito and Bael have been squatting in."

I was perched on the edge of her desk, which Cythera never approved of, but she seemed so preoccupied that she didn't complain.

"Roland said Carlito and Bael didn't leave the house that night after they got in." Zandra sat in a chair on the opposite side of the desk. "I took a good look at his notepad, and he records all his neighbors' movements. He must sit by the window day and night watching their comings and goings."

"It's not the information we wanted, but we can't ignore it," Cythera said. "We have to discount Carlito and Bael as suspects."

"Are you letting Bael go?" I asked.

"I can't keep him any longer. I'll get someone working on his release paperwork, but he's not getting away with fighting us or destroying my wedding board." She stood and strode out of the room, her shoulders slumped.

"Juno, what are you doing?" Zandra glanced over her shoulder to see where Cythera was as I crept across her desk.

"I want to speak to the eyewitness. We need to hear his story." I rifled quickly through the papers on Cythera's desk. There were several reports on boring strategy improvements, but I quickly located the file for Doyle's murder.

"You'd better hurry. Cythera will toss you out if she catches you snooping."

"It's not our fault Cythera isn't sharing all the information."

"Perhaps Brodie doesn't want her to. He's supposed to be in charge."

"Yet, he's vanished. Most likely working to ensure Finn looks guilty." I pushed aside more reports. "We must see the witness."

Zandra kept watch at the door. "Cythera's probably worried you'll interrogate him and force him to change his mind."

"He'll change his mind if he's lying. Here it is. Rembrandt Flicker. I don't know him. Maybe he's a new resident in Crimson Cove, like Roland?"

"We'll look into it. Make sure those papers are back exactly as you found them, or Cythera will know you've been poking around."

I carefully set everything back in place and was back on the edge of the desk when Cythera returned.

"There's no point in either of you hanging around," she said.

"We do need to get to animal control," Zandra said. "We've spent all morning on this, and Barney will be wondering where we are."

"Go. I'll keep you informed if I have any news."

We hurried through the office and out the main doors. When we entered animal control, voices drifted out of Barney's office, so we headed in that direction. Barney sat behind his desk, and Ember Dreamscape and Sammy sat in chairs on the other side of the desk. They wore serious expressions, although Sammy chirruped a greeting when he saw us.

Barney looked up as Zandra tapped on the door, and he smiled a greeting.

"Sorry we're late. We were following a lead in Finn's investigation," Zandra said.

He waved away the comment. "Direct your attention to that. It's an awful business. I don't believe for one second Finn's a killer."

I hopped onto the seat Sammy was in and nuzzled him. "What's going on here?"

"More last-minute trial prep," Sammy said. "Tinkerbell and Bilious are arriving soon too."

"Feeling confident?" I asked.

"We'll make Gaian and Lila pay," Ember said. "They're going away for a long time."

"We'll make sure of it," Barney said. "How is Finn doing?"

"Not great." Zandra leaned against the wall. "Everyone's worried. The more evidence we find, the less positive it's looking for him."

"Then you need a distraction," Barney said. "And I have just the case for you. It requires expert attention."

"Then we arrived at the right time," I said. "What have you got for us?"

He lifted a report sheet off his desk. "It's a worrying statement, and I'm hoping nothing comes of it, but there's been a sighting of a dragon on the town border."

I masked my surprise by washing my face with one paw. "We don't get many dragons around here. There are no local dragon groups within fifty miles of Crimson Cove."

"I was wondering if it was injured. They don't lurk on the ground for long unless there's something wrong with them." Barney handed the information to Zandra. "Could you take a look? It could simply be that someone got startled and made a mistake. But there have been odd things going on around town recently."

I jumped onto Zandra's shoulder and read the report. "What kind of odd things?"

"Scorch marks on buildings and multiple garbage fires. And a few people have seen a white-scaled creature that looks like a small dragon."

"Those reports are coming in here?" Zandra's head whipped up. "I've not seen anything."

"Nothing official, not yet," Barney said, "but I heard a few rumors when I was having a drink the other evening. It could have been the booze talking, but it made me wonder if we've got something rogue hanging around."

"We'll get onto it right away," I said. "Good luck with the trial prep."

Zandra hurried out of the office, the report clutched in one hand. "This is bad. If there's a dragon stationed in Crimson Cove, then the dragons know the hatchling is here. They must be searching for her."

I nodded. "And they're about to make their move. We really are out of time. Let's investigate and see if we can make a deal before it's too late."

***

My paws ached, my stomach grumbled, and there was no sign of any dragon lurking on the town border.

"We've been this way already." Zandra trudged behind me, her head down and pace slow.

"The dragon may not be staying in one area." I dodged around a pile of rocks and sniffed at the dirt. We'd been looking for hours and hadn't had a single sighting of anything that could be dragon-related. No dropped scales or evidence of a dragon kill. Not even a pile of dung. And location spells were proving useless. If there was a dragon here, it was doing an incredible job of keeping itself concealed.

"We're wasting our time," Zandra said. "I've cast a dozen spells to see if I can find this thing, and it's not out here. Whoever sent in that report is an idiot. A time-wasting idiot."

"We can't assume that. If a dragon is in Crimson Cove, it's here for Finn, and we can't let them take him."

"So, we're going up against a full-grown dragon now, are we? Good luck with that."

I looked up at her miserable face and sighed. "It's getting late, and we've been walking for hours. Let's take a break."

Zandra headed to the nearest tree stump and slumped down onto it.

I joined her, wriggled onto her lap, and leaned my head against her chest. "I know you're worried about Finn, so am I, but we will figure out what happened to Doyle. And Finn's memory could return. He must have the answer to this puzzle lodged in there somewhere."

She scratched between my ears. "Sorry for being snappy. You're right. I'm terrified that Finn could be involved. We've seen him when he goes into full demon mode. He has no control. We've had to use all our power to take him down at times."

"But he's been better recently," I said.

"His long-lost dad riding into town must have unsettled him. Stirred up his demon side."

I leaned against her, saying nothing and closing my eyes. We were both anxious about Finn and taking it out on each other. "We have a lot on our minds. Finn, the dragon hatchling, the upcoming trial, even the wedding stress is rubbing off on us. And I haven't had a chance to spend time with Sammy or go squirrel hunting properly in ages."

"You're happy Sammy's back, though?" Zandra asked. "It must have taken you a while to get used to his new look."

"I am. And the external is never as important as a person's character. We're learning about each other all over again." I looked up at her. "Have you asked Randal to the wedding yet?"

"With everything that's going on, I haven't even thought about a date for the wedding." She sighed. "Are we lost causes? We always put everyone else first, so we miss out on happiness?"

"We're happy most of the time, and I get an immense amount of satisfaction when the bad guys get put away. And I know you do. There's nothing more satisfying than seeing justice served."

"Yeah, I guess. But sometimes, I sort of wish we could go back to the old days before we moved to Crimson Cove."

"When you were being bossed around by Tempest and unsure how you fit into the Crypt witch family situation? Did that bring you joy?"

Zandra sighed again. "No, but my life was simpler. At least getting ordered around by Tempest kept me focused."

"I can't agree. You had little control over your magic, you were so unsure of your abilities that you rarely used them, and you didn't even know whether you wanted to be a part of that family. And you were always worrying about your mother."

Zandra was quiet for a moment. "I was. I can't believe how much has changed. I mean, literally changed. Being a ghoul suits her, though. And she's happy with Joel. She's never stayed with the same guy for such a long time."

"It's not an outcome I would have ever predicted for her, but it works," I said. "And we aren't lost causes. We'll only be that if we give up. That's when failure happens. And we aren't failing Finn." I cocked my head. "Did you hear that?"

"No. I was too busy listening to your lecture." She ruffled my fur, a grin on her face.

"I thought I heard something moving around." I climbed off Zandra's lap and took a few steps away from her. There was a faint rustle close by.

"You think you've found the dragon?"

I shook my head. "It's too quiet for that. But there's something out here."

"You'd better not be leading me on a squirrel hunt."

I chuckled softly. That would be a joy, taking down a monstrous tree rat with Zandra by my side. I kept creeping through the foliage, getting closer to the noise. There was more rustling, and twigs broke.

We entered a small clearing and discovered a tent. Sitting outside that tent was a lone male camper.

His head jerked up as he saw us approaching. "Oh! I figured I was all alone out here. You don't look like you're camping. Walking the... cat?" He was a tall, thin man with a shaggy haircut and a blond beard.

"We were looking for something," I said, before making the introductions. "And you are?"

"I'm Rembrandt Flicker. What are you looking for?"

I drew in a breath. "You're Rembrandt? The camper who witnessed Doyle's murder?"

His mouth opened, and he blinked rapidly. "Yes! How do you know that?"

"We work with Angel Force," Zandra said. "We're trying to figure out what happened that night."

Rembrandt looked at his small campfire. "Well, I gave my statement to the angels. Haven't you read it?"

"We know what you witnessed," Zandra said.

"Talk us through it." I marched toward him, magic flickering across my fur.

He jerked back, his expression one of surprise. "I... I don't have anything else to add to my original statement."

"Let's hear it again. We need to know everything."

Zandra joined me, her hands on her hips. "We don't mean to be intense, but it's a close friend who's been accused of murdering Doyle. We can't believe he did it."

Sympathy entered Rembrandt's eyes. "I'm sorry to hear that. That must be difficult for you. Would you like tea? I'm just boiling water."

"No tea." I reined in my frustration. It wouldn't do to scare Rembrandt away before getting the information out of him. "But we do want answers. And we'd be grateful if you could talk us through what you saw that night, just in case you missed something."

Rembrandt lifted a stick and prodded at the flames. "Of course, if it'll bring you comfort. But my eyes didn't deceive me."

"What are you doing out here?" I asked.

"I'm a fan of wild camping. I prefer camping in nature rather than going to an organized campsite. It's cheaper, apart from anything else, and I enjoy getting back to nature."

"If you don't mind me asking, what kind of magic do you use?" Zandra asked.

"I'm a shapeshifter. Nothing fancy, though. I'm a beaver shifter. I love being near water, but any kind of wild space brings me to life. I had a few weeks off work and planned a walking tour. This is the last leg of my journey."

"What did you see the night Doyle was murdered?" I asked.

"I'd arrived in Crimson Cove and decided to stay for a few days. I like to relax at the end of a walk and give my body a rest. It was late, but I'd picked up supplies, so I'd have something to eat before bed. I was walking past that house when I heard an explosion, so I took a look."

"What did you see?" Zandra asked.

"Flames inside the house! I hurried along the driveway and peered through the window. And that's when I saw it. The angel was attacking the demon. Well, he was an angel at first, but then all this red energy flared up, and he changed. He became a demon, too. I've heard of angel-demon hybrids, but it was the first time I'd seen one."

"You got a good look at the angel before he changed?" I asked.

"Yes. And I gave my description to Angel Force. He was a handsome angel, but not a typical blond. His hair was darker, more of a sandy brown. He was still handsome, mind you. I've yet to meet an angel who doesn't look like a bombshell, though."

I gulped down my panic. There was only one sandy-haired angel working at Angel Force. "What happened next?"

"The angel who turned into a demon tried to incinerate the other one. It was intense and terrifying to watch. If I could have done anything to stop them or help, I would have, but my powers lie in helping nature. If I'd interfered, he'd have killed me, too."

"Why didn't you report the attack straightaway?" I asked. "It happened late at night, but according to the angels, you didn't report it until the following morning."

"I was scared! I stood there for several minutes watching the fight, and I became paranoid and convinced I'd been seen. When the angel-demon killed the other one, I ran. But my conscience wouldn't let me forget what I saw. I lay awake all night worrying, convinced the demon was creeping toward my tent. As soon as it was dawn, I hurried back to town and found the angels." Rembrandt lowered his gaze. "I know I did wrong by not coming forward immediately."

"Did the demon you saw being attacked fight back?" I asked.

"Yes. It was brutal and scary."

"So, the demon attacked the angel," I said. "Did he injure him? Maybe the angel had to protect himself, so it was self-defense."

"There were fists and flames flying all over the place. It was so dazzling that there were times when I couldn't see properly. I'm unsure who threw the first blow. I missed the start of the fight."

"Could you have missed someone else being there?" Zandra asked.

"Maybe. I don't know about that, though. I watched for a while and saw no one else enter the room. It was just the two of them fighting."

"And you saw Finn murder the demon?" I asked. "This is really important. Finn's guilt is resting on your testimony."

Rembrandt didn't speak for some time as he prodded at the fire. "I'm so sorry, but your friend did this. The blast of flame that engulfed the demon was astonishing. He meant to kill him. It was no accident. The demon was talking to Finn, holding out his hands and trying to make him stop, but he kept attacking. He was out of control."

We went quiet. Rembrandt appeared to be a normal guy, and his statement sounded genuine, but I still couldn't believe it.

"Did you have anything to drink?" I asked.

"There's tea. You said you didn't want any, though."

"No, I mean, that night. Were you drinking?"

He shook his head. "Oh! No, I don't drink. I get terrible hangovers, and I like a clear head when I walk so I can enjoy as much of nature as possible."

"What about using something more natural?" I asked, scrabbling around to find a hole in his statement. "There are plenty of natural herbs and mushrooms that give a... pleasant effect. Mellow a person out. Sometimes make them hallucinate."

Rembrandt let out a gentle sigh. "I know why you're asking, but I don't use anything like that either. I'm a simple beaver shifter. I like being outside and spending time on my own. I've never gotten in trouble with Angel Force, and I intend to keep it that way. I regret not coming forward as soon as possible, but even if the angels had gone to that house earlier, they'd have been too late to save the demon."

"Is this your first visit to Crimson Cove?" Zandra asked.

Rembrandt nodded. "I like to vary my routes and see new places. You have a nice town."

"Do you know anyone who lives here?"

"No, I don't have many friends. I keep to myself as much as possible. My plan was to walk here, and since it's the last leg of my journey, take a few days to recover and then return home."

"Where is home?" I asked.

He took the kettle off the flames and poured water into a tin mug. "I doubt you've heard of it. It's a tiny place called Chelmer Lee. It's a long way from here. Nothing much happens there, but there are lots of good walking routes, so I like it."

"You're planning on walking all that way back home?" Zandra asked.

"No, I treat myself at the end of every trip and buy a translocation spell. It's not the kind of power

I have, but it's not an expensive spell, and it's a nice way to end an adventure. Are you sure you don't want tea?"

"No, thanks. We'll pass," Zandra said. She looked at me and shrugged.

"I'm really very sorry about what's going on with your friend, and I wish I had better news to tell you," Rembrandt said. "I hope you find what you're looking for."

"Thanks. So do we." We left him to his tea and trudged back through the forest.

"I hate to say this, but he sounded legit," Zandra said. "I couldn't find a hole in his story."

"Same here." My paws felt so heavy I could barely pick them up.

Could Finn have really done this?

Chapter 14

Kitten impossible

"Juno, take a break." Zandra lay across our bed in the basement apartment we rented in Vorana's house. "If there's any news about the trial, Sammy will let you know."

"Everything feels wrong." I paced the length of the basement and back again. After speaking to Rembrandt yesterday and getting the worst news from him, I didn't need more problems, but the trial to convict Gaian and Lila was taking so long. I'd assumed with all the evidence against them, the judge would decide by the end of the morning, but that had come and gone. We'd worked all day, and were back home, fretting.

Well, I was fretting. Zandra was attempting to doze.

"There was a lot of evidence to go through," Zandra said. "Gaian and Lila spent months forming their plans to take over Crimson Cove, and they weren't the only ones involved. The judge needs to hear everyone's statements, and the jury needs time to consider the evidence."

"They'd better not change their minds about Sammy's sentence," I said. "He's almost a free cat, and I'll be devastated if they put him away when he's worked so hard to reform."

"The angels won't change their minds now," Zandra said. "It would take too long. It took them long enough to decide about his final sentence. He'll be out before you know it."

"And what about the sighting of the dragon in the woods?" I stomped around some more. "There was nothing there, but I can well believe they're closing in on Finn. Everything feels out of place."

"Yeah, the dragon is a problem. Maybe Finn's better off behind bars for now," Zandra said. "The dragons will think twice before attacking a branch of Angel Force."

"But they will attack when they know for certain he's involved with hiding the hatchling."

"Hey, you two! Stop lurking down there and come up and be sociable." Vorana's voice carried down the stairs.

"I don't feel like being sociable," I muttered.

"We should go up. Vorana will have treats." Zandra rolled off the bed and stood. She crouched in front of me and scratched under my chin in my favorite spot. "I know you're worried, and you have every right to be, but it's not like you to think so negatively."

"I'm trying hard not to, but I'm so worried for Sammy. I just got him back. What if I lose him again because of some lie Gaian or Lila tells?"

Zandra scooped me up and snuggled me against her chest. "If that happens, we'll make it our personal mission to ensure Gaian and Lila pay. We know plenty of spells that'll make them sorry they ever met us."

"We'll obliterate them," I grumbled.

Zandra chuckled. "We could do some minor obliterating."

"Hurry! Sorcha can't decide," Vorana called out. "It's important."

"We're coming!" Zandra yelled as she hurried to the stairs and dashed up them. "What's the emergency?"

Vorana stood in front of us at the top of the stairs, wearing a stunning pale peach dress, the hemline sweeping the floor. She twirled. "What do you think?"

"You look nice," I said.

She wrinkled her nose. "I need more than nice. We're trying on outfits for Cythera and Maverick's wedding. We've got a dozen to choose from, and I can't decide on any of them. Sorcha looks gorgeous in everything, though. Those curves!" Vorana fanned her face.

"You called us up here to look at dresses?" Zandra scowled.

"Yes! And you're trying some on, too." Vorana tugged on Zandra's elbow. "I'm determined to get you to that wedding wearing something other than black. Or denim."

My mood lifted a fraction at Vorana's enthusiasm as she cajoled Zandra along the hallway and up the stairs to her bedroom.

"I can wear black to a wedding," Zandra said. "There's no law against it."

"No! We're all going to look fabulous in lots of color," Vorana said. "You never know, my dream guy could be at the wedding."

"If he's your dream guy, you could wear a cloth sack, and he'd still adore you." I hopped out of Zandra's arms and onto the bed, where Sage was lounging with her eyes half-shut.

She grunted a greeting at me. "The baby is sulking under the bed after I told her off."

"Oh dear. What's she done this time?" I peered under the bed to see the hatchling curled in the corner, her eyes shut.

"She burped in my face and almost singed off my whiskers."

"Your whiskers look fine to me."

"It was a near miss. If she'd been gassy, I'd have been incinerated." Sage twitched an ear. "You here for the fashion show?"

I nodded as I settled in beside her. My mood continued to lift as Vorana and Sorcha encouraged Zandra out of her clothes and then held up a variety of beautiful dresses. Zandra hated them all, but she was never a fan of anything floaty, frilly, or colorful.

"I'm not in the mood for trying on clothes," Zandra said. "And I can't think about the wedding with everything that's going on."

Vorana lowered the pretty red dress she'd been encouraging Zandra to wear. "We're all worried about Finn, but there's nothing we can do at the moment. Why be miserable for no reason? Until we have more to go on, we shouldn't dwell on a gloomy outcome."

"We must be missing something," Zandra said. "But every time we find something new, it leads straight back to Finn."

"It is a shock," Sorcha said, a note of caution in her voice. "I hate to say this, but Finn has been struggling recently."

"He's a good guy," I said. "He wouldn't do this."

"Finn has a lot on his plate, though. His full-time job at Angel Force, the animal sanctuary getting so busy and not having enough volunteers, losing that patron when it turned out she was a killer. And now the hatchling testing her boundaries." Sorcha pointed at the bed. "Finn's a capable guy, but we all have our limits."

"Those limits don't involve murder," I said. "We haven't even spoken to all the suspects. We have Doyle's demon lady friends to question. Where are they? And where is Brodie? He's supposed to be finding evidence, but I haven't seen him since we left him at the bar with a burger. He'd better not be lazing about while Finn's innocence hangs in the balance."

Vorana busied herself in her closet. "Is Brodie the big angel with the steel-tipped wings?"

"How'd you know that?" Zandra shooed Sorcha away as she tried to do something with her hair.

"Um... well, a Brodie, and I'm not saying it's the same one, has been coming into the bookstore a lot, recently. He said he's here for business. I didn't realize he was involved in the case."

I growled. "He's been flirting with you instead of freeing Finn?"

"No! No flirting." Vorana blushed. "If I'd known who he was, I'd have given him a piece of my mind."

"There's been plenty of flirting," Sage said. "He's too smooth for my liking. And I know he's a fighter. He has scars. And you don't get steel wing tips to go dancing in."

"Next time I see him, we're having words." I wasn't happy the angel leading on this investigation was more interested in getting a date than a conviction.

"Oh! Don't be hard on him. Brodie's not been in the store all the time," Vorana said. "He mentioned something about visiting some demons. Maybe he meant Doyle's girlfriends."

"The angels must have questioned all the suspects by now." Sorcha modeled another dress.

"Not those two. At least not as far as we know. They've disappeared," I said. "They must be hiding because they're guilty. We should look for them, not try on dresses. Although you all look lovely."

"I look ridiculous." Zandra stared down at the blue dress she'd been forced into by Sorcha. "And don't even think about offering me matching heels."

"Just so long as you're not in those stomping boots you always wear, I'm prepared to compromise," Vorana said. "I've got some pretty flats you can borrow. We're the same size."

"Don't try to stop Vorana," Sage whispered. "She loves dressing people up."

"I know. I've seen the outfits she puts you in," I said.

"It's such a humiliation, but I wear them because they make her happy. And we're here to make sure our witches are always smiling, even though we look ludicrous."

"Don't think I forgot you two." Vorana strode over to a bag and rifled inside it. She brought out two pretty sparkling red neckties. "I got these specially made for you."

"We need to focus on Finn." I turned my head away. I couldn't get out of this loop of misery I found myself stuck in.

Vorana crouched by the bed. "Why not have five minutes of joy with us before you get back to the sleuthing? Sage is decorating her harness with sparkles, so you could help her pick out what she wants to use."

Sage lifted her head. "I am? When did we agree on that?"

Vorana chuckled as she clipped the necktie around Sage's throat. "You want to look fabulous at the wedding, don't you?"

"I guess. Although all this hassle for one day is excessive." Sage watched as Vorana held out the necktie for me to sniff.

"Want to try it, Juno?" Vorana asked.

It looked beautiful, and I didn't want to hurt Vorana's feelings by saying no. "Make sure it's not too tight."

Vorana carefully clipped the necktie around my neck and adjusted it until it hung right. She stood back and clasped her hands together. "You both look adorable. You'll be the center of attention at the wedding."

"That'll thrill Cythera. She keeps warning us not to embarrass her." I stood and admired my reflection in a mirror. It was a lovely necktie, and the gems made my eyes gleam. I sighed and settled back on the bed. My heart wasn't in this. I had too much else on my mind, and I couldn't focus.

Sage nudged me with her head. "Sammy will be here any second. Chill."

"I'm trying. But I'm... I'm worried. About all of this." I settled back on the bed with Sage and watched Sorcha and Vorana tussle with Zandra to get her out of the blue dress and into something a little less fitted. I had half an ear on the door, hoping I'd hear Sammy arrive.

"It'll be okay," Sage said. "Even if it isn't, we'll find a workaround."

"We always do. But I can't relax until I know what happened at the trial." I jumped off the bed, walked to the window, and rested my front paws on the sill to peer into the street. My heart skipped a joyful beat. Sammy was striding down the road. And he wasn't alone. Tinkerbell, Bilious, Ember, and Barney were with him.

"They're back!" I dashed out of the bedroom and raced down the stairs. I was so eager to get to Sammy that I fumbled the door handle several times before I got it open.

I bolted toward him. The second he spotted me, his tail lifted, and he ran at me. We met in a leap, and he caught me. We rolled on the ground over and over. I was so pleased to see him.

"We won," he said as he lay on his back, his belly exposed in a show of submission.

"Gaian and Lila have been locked up?" I licked his face.

"They have." Barney joined us with the others, Ember settled on his shoulder. "They'll never see freedom again."

"It was a fascinating day," Bilious said, his face lit by a brilliant inner light only the higher angels radiated. "This dour-faced elderly warlock sat in a chair and stared at us for hours while people talked. I was worried he'd dozed off at one point, but he seemed to know what he was talking about when he made his judgment."

"I'm so pleased to have you back," I said to Sammy. "I was worried something might have gone wrong when you didn't return after lunch."

"There were a few delays. Gaian kept being a jerk, and they had to clear the courtroom several times because he got so aggressive."

I hissed softly. "At least he got what he deserved."

"Hey! Come in, all of you. Juno, I hope you haven't wrinkled your necktie." Vorana stood by the open front door of her house, waving everyone inside. "I'm assuming it's good news."

"The best news," Barney said with a broad smile.

She grinned. "I was hoping you'd say that. I've got champagne chilling in the fridge and food so we can celebrate."

Everyone hurried to Vorana's house and went into the kitchen, talking excitedly about the trial. Vorana unclipped my necktie and brushed off the dust.

Zandra appeared a few minutes later, dressed in her usual outfit of jeans and a T-shirt. She smiled when she saw Sammy. "I take it congratulations are in order?"

He nodded. "It feels great to be free. Well, almost free. I need to do my community service, but I'm more than willing to do that."

"We've got a lot of catching up to do." I leaned against him, purring, delighting in the love and friendship that surrounded us.

I looked around the group as Vorana poured the champagne and placed delicious-looking nibbles on the kitchen table. Someone was missing. Finn should be here. He'd been involved in the investigation that led to Gaian and Lila's arrest. He may have been trapped inside a room and gravely injured while I solved the mystery with Zandra, but he'd still been a part of it.

"Is something wrong?" Sammy asked.

"Not with you. You're perfect. But I need to help Finn. It doesn't feel right we're celebrating while he's stuck in a cell at risk of being charged with a crime he didn't commit."

"What have you got in mind?"

"We still have some of Doyle's friends to question. They've gone to ground, and I consider that suspicious."

"You're going hunting? I'll come with you."

"I'd love that, but you should stay and celebrate with the others. You deserve it," I said.

Sammy looked conflicted. "I want to be with you."

"We can be, soon. As soon as we've gotten Finn free, we'll have more time together. Go celebrate with everybody."

He lowered his head and rested it against mine. "I'll be waiting for you when you get back."

I checked in on Zandra. She was happily sipping champagne and talking to Barney. I snuck away, so as not to disturb the celebration and sour the happy mood. I wasn't giving up on my troubled angel friend. There had to be a way to secure Finn's freedom.

Chapter 15

Dinner time

To save on time, I used a translocation spell to get me to Remus Salamander's opulent mansion in Oak Park Ridge as quickly as possible.

I worked better when I was part of a team, and this mission required expert sniffers to swiftly locate Doyle's female companions. With the use of my amazing booping snooter, Remus's vampires, and Archie's incredible nose, we'd find them faster together.

My timing was perfect since the sun was setting, so the vampires would be up. When I got closer to the mansion, I realized they already had their evening plans underway. The entrance was elaborately decorated with twinkling lights, a large garish death mask in bright red was propped against a boulder, and a row of freshly lit fire sconces glowed as I hurried along the path. They must be having a party. It was hardly a surprise. Remus was the most gregarious vampire I'd ever encountered. The older vampires became grumpy and withdrew from society, but Remus still knew how to enjoy himself.

Lights flicked on in several rooms as I got to the main entrance, and I detected the faint thud of music from inside.

Something slammed against the front door, making me jump. It happened several times, and then there was silence.

"Hello? Is someone there?" I asked.

There was another distant thud from the side of the building, and the ground shook a few seconds later. Archie appeared in a blur of movement as he raced toward me, his tongue hanging out of his enormous mouth.

"Juno! I knew I smelled you. I said to Remus you were outside. I tried to get out of the front door, but then remembered I couldn't open it with my paws, so I went through my hellhound door." He skidded to a halt, attempting to swipe his giant tongue across my head.

I wisely dodged his over-enthusiastic greeting so as not to soil my glorious fur. "Well sniffed out. What's going on here?"

Archie bounced on his paws. "We're having a masquerade ball of the damned."

"Sounds grand."

"Remus describes it as... opulent! Yes. I got that right. All the guests will wear elaborate masks and historical costumes. You should see inside. It's all red and black, with candles everywhere. Remus has been planning the event for months."

"And why did we not receive an invitation to this magnificent affair?" I cocked my head.

He whimpered but then wagged his tail. "Sorry, Juno. It's vampires only tonight. We're hosting special guests from out of town. They'll be here in a few hours. Remus is finishing getting everything set up. There's even a naked room!"

"I'm assuming that description tells me everything I need to know."

Archie huffed out a laugh. "Some of the guests aren't into clothes, so Remus gave them their own room so they can strut around and do whatever they like. I find naked bodies so weird. Where is all the hair? They must always feel cold."

"We're used to our fur, I suppose," I said.

He glanced over his shoulder. "I know it's supposed to be vampires only, but you're so small, I can sneak you in. But we must be careful of our visitors. They're super old-school vampires and will see you as a snack."

"They can try to snack on me, but they'll deeply regret it." I flexed a murder mitten.

Archie hopped playfully from paw to paw. "It'll be even more fun now you're here."

"Sadly, I haven't come to party. Although I left a joyful gathering at Vorana's house. Gaian and Lila have been convicted. The trial is over."

Archie tipped back his head and gave a joyful howl. "Then we have even more reason to celebrate. Sammy is free. And I heard what happened to Tinkerbell. I can't believe she's with a higher angel. And she's being nice to everyone. Who would've thought Tinkerbell could be nice?"

"And you know about Ember?"

Archie nodded. "Bonded with Barney. Another shocker. Still, I suppose if it makes them happy."

"It seems to. Everyone's getting their happily ever after," I said.

Archie's ears lowered. "Not everyone, though. Is that why you're here?"

The front door swept open to reveal Remus Salamander, dressed in an incredible outfit of salmon pink with blue accents. "My adorable bundle of fluffy perfection. It's been a while since you've graced my humble home."

"Greetings, Remus," I said. "Sorry about interrupting the party planning, but I'm here on a matter of urgency."

"How intriguing. Come inside. It'll be safe here for at least two hours, but then I'd advise your hasty departure because you're too delectable to be guaranteed a safe passage when the party is in full swing."

"Archie has already told me about your bloodthirsty visitors." I stopped to admire the entrance hall, which was decorated in vast swatches of red and black fabric, candlelight creating shadowy corners for dark deeds to take place. "They must be special if you're making so much effort."

"I like to think all of my parties are special. But you're right, my visitors are akin to vampire royalty, so I'm pulling out all the stops."

"We have snacks too," Archie said. "Something for everyone. Not just the vampires."

Remus rested a hand on Archie's head as he led us along the main hallway. "I'd never forget your important provisions."

We entered an extravagantly dressed room with several vampires speedily setting up a variety of games.

Remus continued, "Of course, this'll be nothing compared to Cythera and Maverick's wedding. I'm so looking forward to it. Although, I'm hoping for a cloudy day. The bright daylight is so tiring, and I don't want to miss a moment of the glorious event."

"Cythera may be distracted on her big day," I said. "Have you heard what's happening to Finn?"

"I have. Such a shame. He's a charming angel."

"He's being set up," I said. "Everyone who knows Finn knows he wouldn't do this."

Remus paused from inspecting a game that was laid out. "We also know he has a darker side. I heard he had a fight with a demon."

"Allegedly, he was his biological father," I said. "Although I have my doubts about that."

Remus turned to me. "Intriguing. I understood he was a foundling."

"Finn spent his younger years in care," I said. "But suddenly, this demon appeared and claimed to be his father."

"And Finn believed him?"

"He was happy to have this guy in his life."

"But now, this demon is dead," Remus mused, tapping a finger on his chin. "Murdered by his own son."

"That's what everyone is saying, including an eyewitness who saw the whole thing."

"The mystery deepens," Remus said. "Is this eyewitness to be trusted?"

"I've questioned him, and he appears genuine. I was hoping he'd be unreliable, but he said he witnessed the whole thing and gave a worryingly accurate description of Finn."

Remus ambled around the room with Archie beside him, giving the occasional instruction to the beavering vampires. "We've both witnessed Finn when he hasn't been in full control." There was a note of caution in his voice. "Perhaps it was one of those unfortunate occurrences."

"I refuse to believe that," I said. "And you didn't see Finn when he was with Doyle. He was so happy to have met him."

"We should help," Archie said. "I like Finn. He always rubs my belly."

"He's one of my favorite angels, too," Remus said. "Always so cheerful and obliging."

"That's why I'm here," I said. "There are two suspects missing, and I must speak to them."

"Tell me more." Remus swept back into the hallway, and I followed him with Archie.

"Two female demons came to Crimson Cove with Doyle," I said. "Obsidian and Foxglove."

Remus stopped walking and turned to look at me. "Female demons? Go on."

"I only met them for a few minutes, but they could know something important. Ever since Doyle was killed, they've vanished."

"Do you think they committed the crime?"

"It's possible. It wasn't Finn, so it must be someone else connected to Doyle."

"Who does Finn claim murdered his father?" Remus asked.

"That's the problem. He has no memory of the murder. He was knocked out and woke up to find Doyle dead and the room a blazing mess. The most crucial seconds are missing from his memory."

"Unfortunate or convenient?"

I hissed at Remus. "Finn didn't do it."

"Of course he didn't," Archie said. "How can we help?"

"I need your noses to sniff out the missing female demons."

"What if they aren't in Crimson Cove anymore?" Remus asked. "If they committed this terrible crime, they'll be long gone. That's what any level-headed killer would do."

Archie lifted his head. "Don't we have—"

"Not now, Archie," Remus said. "Let's focus on Juno's problem."

"But I thought—"

"Remus, the delivery of A Positive barrels has just arrived. And the circus tent is about to go up on the grounds." An unfamiliar vampire with intense green eyes and sharp cheekbones hurried along the hallway.

"Excellent timing," Remus said. "Juno, you haven't met Denver, have you? He's new to the hive."

I nodded a brief greeting.

"And you'll be delighted to hear he's accompanying the delectable Sorcha to the wedding."

That caught my attention, and I gave Denver a thorough once-over.

His smile faded under my intense scrutiny. "Is something wrong?"

"I'm close friends of Sorcha Creer. You will look after her, won't you?"

"Oh! Of course! She's great."

"Denver spends all of his free time at her café. He's besotted." Remus's smile was indulgent.

Denver ducked his head. "Sorcha's sweet. She's so thoughtful in the way she helps the vampires. I don't do well in daylight, but she's got that room at the back we can use whenever we like. And she has the best blood. She warms it or chills it to the perfect temperature. And she always makes time to chat."

"Sorcha is charming and adorable, but she's also been badly treated recently," I said. "If you break her heart, I'll obliterate you."

Denver gulped and stepped back. "Sure. I mean, I'd never do that. We're still getting to know each other, but I have no plans to mess her around."

"Juno is excellent at keeping her promises," Remus said. "Make sure you behave like a gentleman with Sorcha."

"If you don't, your future will be bleak." I fluffed myself to my largest size and swished a murder mitten through the air.

"Got it. I'll be on my best behavior," Denver said swiftly.

"Go oversee the blood delivery then meet me outside. I'll join you when they're lifting the tent," Remus said.

Denver nodded and dashed away.

"Do you trust him?" I asked Remus.

"Denver wouldn't be a member of my hive if I didn't have absolute trust in him," Remus said.

I nodded. Remus could be as slippery as an oil-soaked eel wrapped in silk, but he'd never put a friend in harm's way.

"Shouldn't we tell Juno?" Archie was staring hard at Remus.

"Tell me what? Is it something about Denver? Should Sorcha not take him to the wedding?" I asked.

"It's nothing. Just a strange coincidence." Remus turned away. "Would you like to see the circus tent?"

I narrowed my eyes at his back. "I'm not a fan of convenient coincidences. What's going on?"

"You should tell her. We could help Finn get free," Archie said.

Remus sighed and turned back to me. "Do we have to? I was so looking forward to playing with them."

"Playing with what?" I asked.

"This way. I have something to show you." Remus turned and strode along the hallway.

"What's going on?" I asked Archie as we hurried behind Remus, dodging fast-moving vampires as they continued the party preparations.

"When you mentioned the female demons, it got me thinking."

"You know them? Have you seen them around town?"

"No! But I think I know where they are."

"Keep up," Remus called over his shoulder. "There's still much to do before this party is perfect." He headed down a set of stone steps and into the cellar. It was brightly lit and warm, so I had no concerns about following him, especially with Archie behind me.

Remus walked to an old wooden door and unlocked it.

"What's behind there?" I asked.

"Hopefully not what you're looking for, or this party won't be as spectacular as I'd anticipated."

I peered into the room as Remus cracked open the door. Inside, chained up and contained in a swirl of magic, were the two missing demons.

Chapter 16

Hidden treasure

I stepped back and glared up at Remus. "What are they doing in there?"

"They're part of the main feast," Remus said. "I found these charming ladies at a loose end, and they said they wanted to party."

"Not like this, jerk face," Obsidian said. "Let us out of here."

"You'll taste so delicious," Remus said. "And I don't want to let my guests down. They've traveled such a long way."

"You take a bite out of me, and I'll snap your neck," Foxglove said, her blonde hair a disheveled mess around her pretty face.

"They have such charming mouths," Remus said with a sigh. "They'd be so entertaining before we feed on them."

"No!" I blocked Remus's path to the demons. "These are the demons that came to town with Doyle. You can't eat them. They could be the key to clearing Finn's name."

"Hey, what's going on? No one's supposed to be down here until... Oh, Remus. I didn't realize it was you." Another vampire appeared on the stairs. "I'm glad I found you. Altruist and Naomi are early, and they're insisting they see you immediately."

"Oh, dear." Remus grimaced as his gaze cut to me. "This could get tricky."

I tensed. "They're your special guests?"

"We are! The most special. We couldn't be any more special if we arrived in a golden carriage pulled by gleaming orange unicorns." A tall, classically handsome vampire with shiny white hair descended the steps, shooing Remus's vampire away with a sweep of his hand.

"Altruist!" Remus swept into a low bow and remained there as the vampire stopped at the bottom of the stairs. He was joined a second later by a stunning pale female with black hair and red-painted lips. Her eye color matched her lips.

"We wanted to surprise you. We have much to discuss. But when we heard raised voices, we wanted to ensure there was no trouble." Altruist's icy gaze swept toward me, and he licked his lips. "Always so thoughtful, providing delicious snacks before the main event."

I hissed at him. "I'm no one's snack. Show some respect."

He looked momentarily startled before his icy indifference returned. "I don't enjoy my food talking back. Remus, where did you get this creature?"

Remus stood slowly from his bow, his body tense. "Forgive me, but Juno is correct. She's a good friend of the hive and under my protection. She is not for us."

"How disappointing. Still, I'm more interested in the main feast." Altruist's eyes drifted to the chained demons who'd fallen silent. They must have sensed the power radiating from this new arrival and his vampire companion, and they were smart enough to keep their mouths shut.

"They're not for you either," I said. "These demons have crucial information in an ongoing murder investigation."

"Murder! Intriguing, but I care nothing for that. Remus promised us a feast and a party, and I intend to have both."

Remus smoothed his blond hair down with one hand. "Another small inconvenience, but I've just learned these demons could be useful to the investigation. Of course, I was about to prepare them for you and the lovely Naomi, but we'll make alternative arrangements. You won't miss out."

Altruist bared his fangs. "I want them. And I'm having them."

"You're not touching them," I said. "A good friend of ours is facing a murder charge, and the information they have could set him free."

Altruist arched a neat brow. "This friend is a vampire?"

"No, but he's a friend of the vampires," I said.

"Then he is of no concern to me. Naomi, take them now. We'll feast in our room."

I remained planted in front of the demons and hissed again, summoning my ancient magic, so it simmered for all to witness. "I'd advise you to think again. Go find yourself another ready meal."

Altruist hissed back, and Naomi joined him. "You're denying me what I desire?"

"It might be a novelty to not get what you want, but you're not having them," I said.

He crouched, and his fingers flexed. Naomi mirrored his movements as they fanned out into a semicircle.

"There's no need for that," Remus said hurriedly. "We have excellent food on tap, and a fresh blood supply has just been delivered. It's being uncorked at this very second."

Altruist was focused on me, ignoring Remus's pleas for peace. "Do you know who I am?"

"I can only conclude that, by asking that question, you're a high-minded, pompous idiot."

"Juno," Remus cautioned. "You must forgive my delicious furry friend. She's not spent much time in the vampire community, so she doesn't understand our ways."

"I've spent enough time with vampires, and I'm aware of your hierarchies. But I'm also aware that respect and decency are not alien to vampires," I said. "Remus didn't know Obsidian and Foxglove were persons of interest in a murder investigation. Otherwise, he would never have taken them. We need to question them."

Altruist hissed. "And I need to drain them dry."

Tension crackled in the air as we glared at each other. Obsidian and Foxglove didn't move, casting wary glances at Altruist and Naomi, knowing their lives were on the line and they were trapped in chains and magic if things didn't go my way.

Altruist's eyes gleamed crimson as he took a step forward. "Move aside, little feline. Those demons are mine."

I arched my back, my claws extending.

Altruist's lips curled into a cruel smile. "Do you honestly believe you can stand against me?"

With a flick of an ear, I summoned a burst of ethereal flames, sending them dancing between my murder mittens.

Altruist's eyes widened for a split second before he leaped forward, his form blurring with supernatural speed. I sidestepped his attack, feeling the rush of air as he passed. Before he could recover, I swiped at him with my murder mittens, raking lines down his arm. He barely deflected the attack, his hand grazing my fur as I spun away.

"You're agile." There was a hint of surprise in his tone as his gaze roved over me. "Old magic, yes?"

"Most likely older than you. And wiser, too." I sent a surge of energy toward him. The cellar trembled as the magic crackled between us, a volatile exchange of power.

Altruist bared his fangs and raised his arm, forming a barrier of darkness to counter my magic. "Naomi, attack!"

Naomi surged forward, her fangs exposed. Before she reached me, Archie jumped and rolled her over. Remus moved so fast I was uncertain what he did, but Naomi was suddenly nowhere to be seen, leaving me with Altruist to deal with.

I clashed with him again, the cellar walls shaking under the strain of our magical duel.

He snarled, his eyes ablaze with determination.

With a swift movement, I lunged, my body transforming mid-air into a shimmering mist. I re-formed behind him, murder mittens ready, and raked them across his back.

Altruist hissed in pain and whirled around, swinging a powerful ball of blood-soaked magic at me. I ducked and rolled, narrowly avoiding the spell.

He roared his anger, and his fist slammed into the stone wall, sending debris flying.

I dipped into my ancient well of power and summoned a swirling vortex of flames around him. Altruist fought the inferno, his features contorted in a mix of rage and agony. With a burst of strength, he shattered the magical flames, emerging from the blaze unscathed. He advanced, his eyes heated with a renewed hunger as he dashed toward Obsidian and Foxglove.

I couldn't let him get them. With a fierce battle meow, I conjured a torrent of shimmering ice daggers, each one homing in on Altruist. He dodged and deflected, but a few of the daggers found their mark, leaving him wounded, although he swiftly healed.

His gaze locked onto mine, his expression a lethal mix of fury and frustration. "I will have my feast."

"And I will make sure my friend is proven innocent!" With a final surge of energy, I summoned a blinding flash of light, momentarily disorienting

Altruist. Seizing the opportunity, I lunged at him, claws extended, aiming for his chest.

Altruist staggered back, his defenses faltering. My claws met resistance as they tore through his clothing. He raised his hand and unleashed a wave of dark vampiric energy.

I leaped aside, narrowly avoiding the toxic blast. As the energy dissipated, I focused my magic into my murder mittens and delivered a powerful strike to his stomach, sending him stumbling back and groaning.

Altruist crashed against the stone wall, his body slumping to the floor. He glared up at me, his once-confident demeanor replaced with a mixture of defeat and anger.

"Altruist! Naomi requires your attention." Remus's voice reverberated with a power few would dare to ignore. "There's something wrong with her."

Altruist hesitated, torn between attempting to beat me and assisting his companion. "Naomi? Did you hurt her?"

"I didn't touch her. She lunged at Juno, but collapsed before she could reach her," Remus said. "She's been unresponsive ever since I caught her."

A faint groan from Naomi reached my ears. What had Remus and Archie done to her?

Altruist frowned as he attempted to get up, but my magical strike had sucked away his energy. "She's been experimenting with intermittent fasting. It weakens her. Bring her to me."

Remus carried a woozy Naomi to Altruist and settled her beside him. "I believe she fainted."

"She's just hungry. Foolish creature. She's older than me and needs regular feeds, but she refuses. Always following the latest fad to cleanse herself."

I moved to guard Obsidian and Foxglove. Altruist noticed and bared his fangs.

Remus stood beside me, Archie guarding him. "This is a simple misunderstanding. Blood has been stirred, but it doesn't need to be spilled. We can find another feast. You may even enjoy hunting with us. I'm certain Naomi would welcome a fresh meal."

Altruist spent a moment whispering to Naomi until her eyes opened. He assisted her to her feet, a look of abject hatred in his eyes as he glared at me. "What manner of creature are you?"

"One you need to show more respect," I said. "I asked nicely to keep the demons, and you ignored me. What did you expect would happen?"

He tugged on his suit jacket to smooth the wrinkles. "Remus has always enjoyed collecting oddities."

Remus slid a glance my way then bowed his head. "I'll admit, my hive of vampires is unique, and I'm proud of them. I consider Juno and her bonded witch honorary members of that hive. As such, I cannot allow you to take these demons." He lifted a hand to stop Altruist from protesting. "If, however, they prove to be of no value to Juno, and we can find them again, we'll be free to do as we desire."

Obsidian inhaled, drawing a breath to voice her unhappiness, but I swiftly glanced at her and shook my head. This truce was tenuous, and a wrong word would start the fighting again. Neither Obsidian nor

Foxglove said anything, but they looked unhappy to be pawns in this negotiation.

"Tell me more about this murder," Altruist said. "I need to know what I'm giving up is worth the sacrifice."

"A valuable member of Angel Force has been accused of murdering a demon claiming to be his father," I said. "However, he's being framed. These demons are suspects. It's even possible they killed the victim."

"Hold on a minute," Obsidian said. "I didn't kill him."

"Neither did I," Foxglove said. "Why would I want Doyle dead? I was dating him."

"I can think of several reasons," I said. "Jealousy, rejection, anger, spite."

Altruist pursed his lips, one arm around Naomi as she swayed on her feet. "The female of the species is so deadly. Beautiful but deadly." He conferred with Naomi for a moment. "Very well. You have my permission to take the demons. I always find their taste sour, anyway."

"You're quite right." Remus approached Obsidian and Naomi. "Of course, if you add the sweetness from a nymph and the salt of a mermaid, you get sweet, sour, and salty all in one. Delicious."

"Not helping here," I murmured to him.

"That would have been a magnificent feast," Altruist said.

Remus hesitated. "Another time?"

Altruist nodded. "We have a business matter to discuss, anyway. The food and party can wait.

Although Naomi must drink something before she faints again."

She looked at her watch and shook her head. "I still have two hours of fasting."

"Tsk, tsk. You're already perfection. No more foolish cleanses. You can't cleanse something that is already flawless."

Naomi kissed Altruist's cheek. "I'll have the cat."

I bristled, and Archie growled.

Altruist huffed out a breath, while Remus chuckled softly behind me. "Let's stick to the blood barrels for now. They don't have such sharp claws."

Naomi pouted but didn't put up a fight.

Remus turned to Obsidian and Foxglove. "If I gift you freedom, will you answer all of Juno's questions?"

"You don't get to command us," Obsidian said.

Foxglove kicked her in the shin, making her yelp. "If you get us out of here and away from Queen Creep and her freaky bloodsucker, we'll answer any questions you like. Isn't that right, Obsidian?"

Obsidian sighed. "Sure. Whatever."

"I have your word?" Remus asked. "Remember, there are plenty of bloodthirsty vampires who desire to drain you if you don't hold up your end of the bargain."

"I said yes!" Obsidian snapped. "Get me out of these chains."

"You'll get no problems from me," Foxglove said. "I want to know what happened to Doyle as much as everyone does."

I nodded at Remus. "Is there a private room we could use?"

He unbound Obsidian and Naomi from the enchanted chains. "Of course. I'll get someone to show you a place you won't be disturbed."

As we left the cellar, we had to walk past Altruist and Naomi, but they only hissed for a few seconds as we ascended the stairs. I took the lead with Archie, Obsidian and Foxglove sandwiched behind us, while Remus took the rear guard.

"Denver," Remus called out as he reached the top of the stairs. Within half a second, Denver had appeared, awaiting his orders. "Please show my guests into the salon. Ensure they're not disturbed."

"Of course. This way." Denver led us along the hallway and into the salon, the walls adorned with rich, dark wood panelling, intricately carved with ornate designs, and lit by expensive chandeliers. Plush velvet couches and armchairs upholstered in shades of burgundy and gold were thoughtfully arranged in conversational groupings.

"Alas, I must leave you." Remus stood in the doorway. "I have an unhappy vampire to placate and his fainting companion to bolster with blood. I'll take them hunting for a new main feast. Killing something will make them happy."

"As long as Altruist doesn't attack any of the residents in Crimson Cove," I said.

"I'll ensure he behaves. I'll leave you in Archie's excellent care." Remus petted Archie on the head then disappeared with Denver.

Once the door was closed and Archie had found a comfy spot on a ruffled rug to settle on, I turned to Obsidian and Foxglove. "Let's start with you," I said to Foxglove.

She didn't look happy but sat on the couch next to Obsidian. "What do you want to know?"

"Why were you in Crimson Cove?" I hopped onto a chair opposite them.

"Doyle invited me along. He thought it would be fun."

"Do you know anybody who lives here?"

She shook her head. "First time visiting. And after this experience, I won't be coming back. Vampires give me the shivers. They're so cold and still, but then, whoosh, they animate. Gross."

"What did you know about Doyle's relationship with Finn?" I asked.

"Nothing! Doyle sprung it on me on our way here. It was a shocker. And I've got to admit, I'm not the maternal type, so I wasn't thrilled to learn he had a kid. But Finn seemed nice, and Doyle wanted him to become a part of his family, so I didn't complain. And I figured he'd soon get bored. It was always hard to keep Doyle interested in anything for long. He liked playing with shiny new things."

Obsidian bared her teeth in a warped smile. "You got that right."

"Was this the first time you'd met Finn?" I asked Foxglove.

"Sure. Like I said, I didn't even know he existed until recently."

Obsidian smirked. "Doyle is hardly an angel, though. It was no surprise to me that he'd planted his wild seed and then abandoned it. I wouldn't be shocked if there were half a dozen brats with a connection to him."

Foxglove ignored her. "Doyle was an outgoing guy, but we were happy together. I'm still in shock that he's gone."

"How long had you been involved with Doyle? I'm assuming it was a romantic relationship," I asked.

"Ages. And we were super happy. We were planning on getting married."

Obsidian snorted a laugh.

"Something you want to say?" Foxglove asked her.

"No, no. You keep talking, and I'll keep shaking my head in disbelief."

Foxglove glared at her. "We were happy. Doyle was an outrageous flirt, but I knew he loved me. We'd even been ring shopping, and I was looking for the perfect ring for him to buy me."

"Did you notice any tension between Doyle and Finn?" I asked.

"A little but nothing bad. I mean, Finn was asking questions about what happened when he was a kid, but I could tell Doyle didn't want to answer when everyone was around. He's a private guy. But I knew he was thinking through his answers to Finn's questions, so I guess that's why he had a boys' night in, just the two of them, so they could hash things out. That's when things went bad."

"Were you at the house that night?" I asked.

"Not for long. We all stopped by. Me, Obsidian, Carlito, and Bael. We had a drink, but Doyle basically told us to shove off, so we all went our separate ways."

"Where did you go? Did you spend the evening together?" I asked.

Foxglove shook her head. "Carlito and Bael went off together. I didn't go with them."

"I don't spend any more time with Foxglove than I have to," Obsidian said. "Her laugh sets my teeth on edge. She sounds like a chain-smoking donkey hacking up a phlegm ball."

"And your perfume is so overpowering that I get sick to my stomach every time I'm around you," Foxglove shot back.

They glared at each other in tense silence for a few seconds.

Archie whimpered.

"So, where did you go?" I asked.

"I got a mani-pedi," Foxglove said. "I wanted to look nice for my guy."

"So late?" I asked.

"Some of those places stay open twenty-four hours and cater to all supernaturals. I found a place in the next town over and went there for some pampering."

"Liar!" Obsidian shoved Foxglove in the shoulder. "There's your killer. She just lied to your fuzzy face."

Chapter 17

Demon fire

"Take that back!" Foxglove spun in her seat. "I was there."

"Show us your toenails," Obsidian said. "If they're as rank as your cheap gel fingernails, then you need to get your money back."

"You're a vicious cow!" Foxglove blasted Obsidian with a fireball.

I hopped onto Archie's back. "Let's allow these ladies to work out their issues while avoiding the demon fire blasts, shall we?"

He happily jogged away and stood in one corner of the room, staring as Obsidian and Foxglove faced off, their eyes locked in a fiery glare.

"You think you can lie and get away with it?" Obsidian sneered, flames flickering in her eyes.

Foxglove's laughter was tinged with a dark edge. "Oh, please. You're jealous because Altruist never paid any attention to you."

Obsidian's hands erupted in flames. "You're the one who can't stand the idea of him being interested in someone else. And believe me, he is."

Foxglove's response was a wave of her hand, conjuring a swirling mist of darkness that countered Obsidian's flames.

Obsidian shrieked her anger, making my toe beans tingle. "It's your twisted version of the truth that's annoying."

The room crackled with energy as their powers clashed, sending sparks of fire and shadows dancing around.

Obsidian shot a burst of flames toward Foxglove, who responded by creating a shield of swirling darkness. The flames sizzled as they met the shadowy barrier, filling the air with the scent of burnt wood.

"You're the one who's always making up stories," Foxglove taunted.

Obsidian's laughter was a wild cackle. "You've been spinning lies about Doyle from day one, especially to yourself. He thought you were ridiculous."

Their powers intensified, sending a shockwave of heat through the room. Furniture toppled, and the air grew thick with smoky shadows.

"Should we summon some vampires to help?" Archie whispered.

"Not yet. I want to know which one of them has been telling lies. They'll stop talking if they have a bigger audience of bloodthirsty vamps," I said.

"You're not going to win, Foxglove," Obsidian growled, her flames burning even hotter.

Foxglove's eyes glinted with determination, and the room crackled with an electric tension as they continued to unleash their powers, testing each other's boundaries. Fire and darkness clashed in a spectacular display, casting wild and shifting shadows against the walls.

I ducked as a rogue flick of demon energy got too close and batted it away with a murder mitten before any fur got singed.

"It sounds like Obsidian knows Foxglove lied," Archie said. "Do you think she's lying because she killed Doyle?"

"One of them isn't telling the truth," I said.

Obsidian's flames intensified, forming a blazing wall that reached toward Foxglove. With a wicked grin, she manipulated the flames into a fiery serpent, hissing and writhing as it lunged toward Foxglove.

But Foxglove was no less skilled. She wove shadows around her, shaping them into tendrils that twisted through the air like living things. The tendrils swirled around the fiery serpent, sapping its strength and causing it to dissipate in a burst of smoke and embers.

Obsidian's eyes narrowed, and her focus shifted. The air vibrated with dark energy, and she unleashed a blast of raw, concentrated darkness, aiming it at Foxglove.

Foxglove summoned fire, creating a vortex that engulfed the dark blast and incinerated it. "Is that all you've got?"

Obsidian's lips curled into a cruel smile. "Oh, you have no idea." She summoned an aura of intense heat around her. The flames grew brighter and hotter, and her form shimmered with an otherworldly fire. She shot forward like a blazing comet, aiming for Foxglove.

Foxglove met the challenge head-on. She embraced the swirling shadows around her, and they coiled, forming a protective barrier.

Archie whined. "We should stop them. Remus has expensive antiques in here that he won't like destroyed, including my portrait treat dispenser."

"I'd forgotten about that wonderful invention," I said. "Let's grab snacks while the ladies work out their problems."

"Are you sure we shouldn't stop the fighting?" Archie glanced at the portrait. "Although, I am hungry."

"Positive. What flavors have you got in your portrait?"

Archie wagged his tail as he hurried to the enormous portrait of Remus and Archie. Treats were always the perfect way to distract him.

The portrait was a gift from Remus and came with an enormous food dispenser concealed behind it. All Archie had to do to get a treat was touch his magnificent nose onto Remus's hand and food appeared.

"I've got roast pheasant and duck, and there's beef in there. Both are delicious."

We spent a few minutes sampling the wonderful treats while the demons attacked each other. I had to save a few antique vases from being shattered when they shot out a rogue flame or blast, but other than that, they were restrained in their attempted obliteration, more intent on gouging each other's eyes out than bringing down the mansion.

"They have nasty tempers," I said to Archie.

"They could have lost control when they were with Doyle and snuffed him out," Archie suggested, around a mouthful of beefy kibble.

I nodded. "An interesting theory. They killed him together. Obsidian and Foxglove ganged up against Doyle and destroyed him. They've demonstrated they have the power to do so."

"No way!" Obsidian shoved Foxglove over and glared at me. "I wouldn't side with this harpy."

Foxglove scrambled to her feet and shoved her back. "And I'd never work with this fruit loop."

"Now that's settled, have you gotten your anger out of your systems, or should we have more snacks?" I asked. "If you need to keep slugging it out, may I request you avoid the Louis the XIV chair?"

Obsidian scowled at Foxglove. "When she starts telling the truth, I'll stop thumping her."

Foxglove patted her hair back into place. "I didn't lie! Doyle told me once that he wanted to marry me. He said if he was the marrying kind, I'd be the first woman he asked."

Obsidian smirked. "You're so naïve, it's almost adorable. Doyle had way too much fun being single to settle for one woman."

"We were together, and he was always telling me I was his special girl," Foxglove said.

"Yeah, just like he told me," Obsidian said on a sigh. "Sugar, we've been played. He was seeing both of us at the same time. He told me I was his special lady, too."

Foxglove stared at her, unblinking

"Neither of you were aware of his complicated romantic entanglements?" I asked.

Foxglove was silent for a few seconds. "Definitely not. Doyle promised me he was seeing no one else."

"You believed him?" Obsidian shook her head. "He told me the same, but I knew better. I've been around Doyle's type before, and they're all false promises and smooth words. He'd have said whatever he needed to say so he got what he wanted from you."

"I... I sometimes wondered about him." Foxglove walked back to the couch and sank into it, and the rest of us followed, settling into our own seats. "He'd tell me he was going somewhere, and when I asked about it, it would be a completely different place or he'd met with different people."

"Getting muddled in his own lies," Obsidian added, patting Foxglove's knee. "He was using you."

"Was he using you, too?" I asked.

"Sure, but I knew what game he was playing, and I was happy to play along for as long as it suited me," Obsidian said.

"It sounds like you didn't have a high opinion of Doyle," I said.

"Doyle was fun. I hung out with him because he went to interesting places and was happy to spend money on me. But I knew never to trust him. He was a lying jerk."

"Doyle told me he hired you to be his debt collector," Foxglove said. "He mentioned nothing about dating you, too."

"That's how we met. He needed a payment collected." Obsidian shrugged. "Sorry to break the bad news, but he'd have never gotten serious with you."

"He was stringing you both along?" I asked.

"And I'm sure he had others," Obsidian said. "Maybe when he invited us to Crimson Cove, he was hoping we'd be his main entertainment. Such an idiot."

Foxglove wrinkled her nose. "I'm kind of glad he's dead. He deserved it. Well done, Finn, you saw straight through his lies and blasted him into tiny pieces."

"We're certain it wasn't Finn," I said. "We've been interviewing everyone who had a connection to Doyle to find out what actually happened."

"I heard it was demon flame that burned him up," Obsidian said. "There's not much else that can kill a demon."

"Beheading works," Foxglove said.

"Doyle's head was firmly attached to his body," I said.

"What about the demons who live here?" Obsidian asked. "You hassling them, too?"

"We have a few demons in Crimson Cove, but they're carefully monitored and always well-behaved," I said. "Did you know that Doyle wanted to reunite with Finn?"

"We talked about nothing important," Obsidian said. "Our relationship was barely a relationship. It must have been over a month since the last time I saw him."

Foxglove swiveled in her seat. "Now who's the liar?"

"What do you mean?" I asked.

"Obsidian thinks I'm not telling the truth, but I saw Doyle with her just last week."

"You stalking hag!" Obsidian shrieked as she shoved Foxglove.

Foxglove grabbed her in a headlock, and they fell to the floor, kicking and screaming, smoke billowing around them.

"Archie, let's teach these ladies how to behave." I lunged at Obsidian, knocking her away from Foxglove with a blast of magic from my murder mittens. I pinned her, shoving her down, until she stopped fighting.

I glanced at Archie. He had Foxglove squashed firmly beneath him.

"You ladies need to stop fighting each other. Doyle was the problem here," I said.

"I saw them together!" Foxglove squeaked out, her voice muffled under Archie's fur.

"Because you're a freaky stalker who can't keep away from me," Obsidian said. "I heard rumors about you. Nasty little obsessive sneak."

"We'll get nowhere by insulting each other. Tell me the facts," I said.

"If you get off me, I'll tell you what I know about Foxglove," Obsidian said.

"Will you behave?" I pressed a murder mitten against her throat.

Obsidian smirked. "If I must, although being the good girl doesn't come naturally."

I looked at Archie and nodded. We released the demons and returned to our seats, although I had a spell prepared if either of them misbehaved

Obsidian and Foxglove exchanged heated glares then a burst of laughter bubbled up from both of them.

"Seriously, we're fighting over Doyle?" Obsidian chuckled. "Why bother?"

Foxglove's laughter grew, and she did indeed sound like an adorable chain-smoking donkey with bronchitis. "Yeah, like two jealous exes who never were. This is ridiculous. I never really trusted him."

Obsidian shook her head, still chuckling. "We know how to make a scene, don't we?"

Foxglove grinned. "At least we're entertaining."

I exchanged an amused glance with Archie.

With a shared smile, the tension faded, and the demons sat together on the couch.

"So, about Doyle..." I focused on Foxglove.

"He told terrible lies. And I caught him out on more than a few, but I always forgave him."

"Yeah, he was a loser who thought he was smarter than he actually was." Obsidian brushed my white fur off her chest. "And I'll admit, I saw Doyle about a week ago. Not for long, though. We had a couple of drinks and fooled around, but then I had to work. It was no big deal."

"It proves you weren't telling the truth." Foxglove lifted a hand as Obsidian huffed smoke in her face. "I'm just saying..."

Obsidian shrugged. "We're both guilty of that."

"I didn't lie about being at the nail bar when Doyle was murdered," Foxglove said. "Although maybe I concealed that I'd followed Doyle because I knew he was hiding things from me."

"That's when you saw him with Obsidian?" I asked.

Foxglove nodded. "I got jealous."

Obsidian pursed her lips and looked away. "And maybe you were telling the truth about being at the nail bar, but they still did a lousy job on your gel tips."

Foxglove inspected her nails. "I'll have to get them redone soon. They didn't seem to know what they were doing."

"You know, for certain, Foxglove was at the nail bar?" I said to Obsidian.

She nodded.

"Oh! And you accuse me of being a stalker. Why are you following me?" Foxglove asked.

"I'm not, you moron! My boss knew I was coming to Crimson Cove, and he had a few debts that needed collecting. One of them was from the nail bar. Since Doyle kicked us out to have a cozy night in with his so-called son, I worked." Obsidian glanced my way. "I freelance as a bounty hunter and do debt collection when the payout is worth it."

I snorted my disbelief. "You were sent to a nail bar to pick up money?"

"It's not a legit nail bar. It's a front for dark magic peddling, so the job paid well."

Foxglove's eyes widened. "I thought it was a weird place. They didn't want to serve me."

"Yeah, maybe do your research better next time," Obsidian said. "You're lucky you didn't get an infection."

I sighed as the women talked about the dubious nail bar and where Foxglove should try next. I'd have to check the legitimacy of the place, but since they were there and alibied for each other, it meant neither of them killed Doyle.

Which left us with the same problem. Who murdered Doyle?

Chapter 18

All is lost?

"They were at the nail bar." Cythera marched into her office, her usually perfect face showing signs of tiredness. "Foxglove was getting something called gel tips, and Obsidian was picking up some money."

Cythera wasn't the only one who was tired. Zandra and I had barely slept last night, worrying about Finn and how we'd get him out of this mess.

Brodie was also there, slouched in a chair and nursing a mug of coffee. "Since Foxglove and Obsidian were at the nail bar at the time of the murder, we rule them out as suspects."

I barely spared him a glance. "I'm surprised you're here. I figured you'd have more book buying to do."

Brodie smirked. "Keeping tabs on me, huh?"

"What else do you expect when our friend's freedom hangs in the balance and you're more interested in flirting with the single ladies of Crimson Cove?"

"I can do both."

"Stop bickering." Cythera sat in her seat, tension radiating off her as she stared at the paperwork in front of her. "Unfortunately, I agree with Brodie. Obsidian and Foxglove are no longer suspects."

"If we discount them, we'll have no suspects left," I said. "Foxglove and Obsidian weren't in Crimson Cove, and Bael and Carlito were getting drunk in the house they invaded. That means we're out of options."

"We have one option," Brodie said.

"No! We've missed someone," I said.

Cythera's wings sagged behind her. "As much as I want to believe that, the eyewitness is credible. Finn fits his description perfectly."

I wrinkled my booping snooter. "We've met Rembrandt. And it pains me to say it, but he's believable."

"How did you..." Cythera glanced at the paperwork on her desk and scowled. "Of course, snooping into things you shouldn't."

"Finn insisted we help, so we needed access to all information sources," I said. "I make no apologies for that. And you shouldn't be angry with us for trying to ensure Finn goes free by questioning the eyewitness."

Cythera mumbled something under her breath. It may have been an apology or a curse, but whatever it was, it left a sour taste in her mouth as her nose crinkled and she flipped aimlessly through papers.

"We've reached the end of the road." Brodie set his mug on Cythera's desk. "I've given you time to investigate while I've done my own digging. All roads lead back to Finn. You know what I have to do."

"Not yet. We need more time. We'll change tactics to find the killer." I stood from my comfortable position on a stack of neat paperwork on Cythera's desk. "We should go back to the crime scene, talk to the suspects again. We can't leave any stone unturned. This is Finn! He's no killer."

Cythera heaved out a sigh. "Brodie's been more than generous in giving us time to investigate."

"He's not been doing his job!" I hissed at Brodie.

"Despite what you think, Brodie has given me daily updates about his progress."

I fluffed my fur. "We should have had those, too."

Zandra nodded. "Finn deserves the best. If you've kept information from us—"

"I haven't," Brodie said. "And I've been asking the same questions as you. Visiting the same people. We've run out of road. I don't want Finn to be guilty any more than you do, but we must stick to the facts and the evidence. Finn and Doyle were alone in that house. The doors and windows were locked, and intensely hot flame killed Doyle."

"What about Finn's injuries?" Zandra asked. "He didn't give them to himself."

"He got into a brawl with his dad," Brodie said. "Doyle was powerful. It would have taken someone with demon energy to injure Finn."

"I refuse to believe it," I said. "Give us another week."

Brodie shook his head. "I wish I could, but I've got my head honcho demanding answers, and I can't stall her any longer. If I don't deliver my report, she'll take over. And no one wants that."

None of us spoke. This was the worst possible outcome. Finn had been the first angel we'd met when we moved to Crimson Cove, and I'd instantly taken to his friendly nature and charm. He'd helped Zandra and me on so many occasions, and we'd done likewise for him. He was a friend, and I trusted him. Which was why I refused to believe he was a killer.

"I'll go speak to him," Cythera said. "Give him the news."

"No, I'll do it," Brodie said. "I'm not pulling rank, but it's hard when a good one turns bad, especially when they're a member of your team."

Cythera looked away, but I didn't miss the rare flash of tears in her eyes. "I had my doubts about opening up Angel Force to hybrids, but Finn proved himself more than worthy. I'm sorry it's come to this."

"It's not your fault." Brodie stood from his seat. "It's this job. You see so much bad stuff that it messes with your head. Finn's not the first angel to snap. And with his fiery temper..."

I hissed out my frustration. This was a mess. If they charged Finn with this murder, the fallout would be enormous. And then there was his animal sanctuary and the dragon hatchling to worry about. Finn was leaving too much behind.

"We'd like a few minutes with Finn," I said.

"I'm sure he'd welcome a friendly face before this goes down." Brodie glanced at Cythera, and she nodded her approval. "I could do with another coffee, anyway."

"Just don't do anything foolish like breaking him out," Cythera said. "I know you don't want this to happen, but interfering with the process will get you both in serious trouble and only make things worse for Finn."

I'd briefly considered an attempt at getting Finn free, but Cythera spoke sense. Life on the run for someone who was a wanted criminal would be a joyless experience and only end in tragedy.

"We just want to talk to him," Zandra said. "We'll behave."

We headed to the cells, the atmosphere in the open-plan office gloomy. The rest of the team realized what was about to happen, and none of them were happy about it.

We reached Finn's cell. He lay on the small cot, his knees up, staring at the ceiling.

"I'm guessing it's time," he said.

"We're not giving up on you," Zandra said. "We'll keep looking for the killer."

"We know you didn't do this," I said.

He sat up slowly and leaned his elbows on his knees. "Thanks for doing everything you could. I know you wouldn't have missed anything, and I know you took this case seriously."

"We still are," I said. "We're not finished."

"If you're here looking so glum, I imagine Cythera is." Finn looked weary. "She's been to see me every day and give me updates. She even snuck me extra food. When she's nice to you, you know there's serious trouble coming your way."

"She's unhappy about this outcome, too," Zandra said.

"Sure, she is, but it's not just me she has to worry about," Finn said. "She's looking after the whole team. And she's about to get married! Cythera should focus on that, not one of her deadbeat team members who screwed things up."

"Cythera wouldn't let a little thing like her marriage distract her from ensuring your freedom," I said. "She even told Maverick that murder comes before marriage."

Finn softly laughed. "How did he take that?"

"In his usual affable way," I said.

"Good for him. Maverick is just what Cythera needs," he said. "He's loosened her up."

No one spoke for a moment, and my heart felt lodged in my throat as Finn sat in a cloud of dejection and defeat.

"I need to ask you a favor," Finn said. "Look after the hatchling for me."

Zandra opened her mouth then snapped it shut. She glanced down at me and shook her head.

Finn pinched the bridge of his nose. "Everything was on track. I had my dad back. The dragons had stopped lurking around and tracking me, and even the sanctuary was calmer. Everything was great, but then this happened. It's so unfair. It's like I've been cursed."

"You haven't. And we still haven't given up on you. This is just... unfortunate," I said.

"You should. Stay as far away from me as possible. Everything I touch goes bad."

"Far from it," I said. "The hatchling has thrived under your care. The unloved animals of the area have a safe space to go because of you, and Crimson Cove is a safer place since you've been working here."

"Now that's all gone. And I'm the one behind bars." Finn looked up at us. "I know I'm asking the impossible with the hatchling, but she likes you, Juno. She's got a safe place with you for now."

"We'll do what we can for her," Zandra said. "But she needs to be with her own kind, so she knows how to become an amazing dragon."

Finn pursed his lips then exhaled hard through his nose. "I guess I have no say over what happens to her now. But we were happy together. I've been taking good care of her. I know I've not always done the best job, but it's hard work being a single parent."

"We'll do what's right for her," I said. "It's the best offer you're getting."

"I'll take it." The pain in his eyes when he looked up hurt my heart. "I won't be able to see her again, will I?"

"Best if you don't," I said. "It would be impossible to sneak her in here, and Cythera isn't letting you loose."

The main door to the cells opened, and Brodie appeared. He tapped a finger against his wrist. Our time was up.

Finn stood and walked over to us. "Before you go, I need you to do me one more thing. Look out for Torrin. He's been going through a tough time with a girlfriend. Her parents don't approve of them being together, and I've been helping him figure things out. It's a complicated situation."

"That's what your secret conversations have been about?" I asked.

Finn nodded. "Torrin didn't want anyone else to know. I've been doing what I can for him, but he's kind of a mess. He's fallen hard for her, and he's not letting go, even though her parents are threatening to kill him."

"Sounds like an interesting family she's come from," Zandra said. "What are they, mafia?"

"Nothing like that. Just watch out for Torrin. The last time I spoke to him, he said someone had broken into his repair shop. He reckoned they were looking for him, but he was out at the time on a pickup. He can be a headstrong idiot, but his heart is in the right place, and he'd lay down his life to protect this woman."

"We'll watch over him," Zandra said. "You focus on looking after yourself. And you never know, your memory could come back. You could remember those important moments from that night. Then you'd be a free angel."

"Yeah, I don't see that happening any time soon."

Brodie walked over. "Let's get this over with, shall we, Finn?"

Chapter 19

What if...

The hatchling lay on her stomach next to my chair. Just like the rest of us, she had no appetite after hearing the news that Finn was to spend the rest of his days behind bars.

"I'm still in shock," Vorana said. She sat at the head of the table in her kitchen. We were there, along with Sage and Sorcha. None of us were eating dinner. Even the temptingly moist, flaky white fish on my plate couldn't summon my appetite. I was grieving for Finn's freedom.

"We should go back to the start," I said. "Talk to all the suspects again, visit the crime scene, discover the important clue that we missed that'll solve this mystery."

"What clue do you need?" Sorcha asked. "From what I've heard, the house where the fight went down was a charred mess. Surely, any clues would have gone up in flames."

"And Brodie talked to the neighbors," Zandra said. "No one saw anyone creep into the house to cause trouble for Finn and Doyle."

We'd grilled Brodie after he'd charged Finn to find any weaknesses in the evidence he'd gathered, but everything he told us only sealed Finn's guilt over and over.

The hatchling sighed and whimpered.

I hopped from my seat and rested my head on top of hers. "You'll see Finn again soon. We're not giving up on him. And if the worst happens, we'll find a way for you to visit him."

"He'd hate this." Vorana threw down her fork. "He wouldn't want us moping and miserable because of what's happening to him."

I nodded. "Finn always loved any excuse for a party."

Vorana shoved back her seat. "We should go to the bar and have a drink."

"I don't want to drink," Zandra said.

"For Finn. It'll strengthen our resolve. And didn't you say Finn wanted you to look in on Torrin?" Vorana asked. "We'll pass his repair shop on the way to the bar."

"I'm also not in the mood to go out," I said. "I'll stay with the hatchling."

"She's overdue a nap," Vorana said. "And I've got a new fireproof pen for her to try. She'll feel better when she's had some sleep."

"I'll still stay," I said.

Vorana shook her head as she stood. "I've got the monitor, and she's got her cozy bed. She'll sleep for hours." She crouched beside me. "You did your best. Don't let Finn down now by sinking into depression."

I looked up at Zandra, and she shrugged. "We said we'd see how Torrin was doing."

"Exactly! Finn would want us raising a drink in support of his innocence," Vorana said. "And we've got the wedding to look forward to."

"Is it something to look forward to, or will it be torture?" Zandra asked. "The number of dresses you forced me into suggests the latter option."

Vorana smiled at her. "You looked gorgeous in all of those dresses. We'll all look gorgeous on the wedding day. Which, in case you've all forgotten, is less than two days away."

"So soon? I really have lost track of time," I said.

"You've got to be there so you can watch Cythera scowl as she stomps down the aisle," Sorcha said.

"She'll smile," I said. "Cythera doesn't like to admit it, but she has a soft spot for Maverick. And he adores her. It'll be nice to see them finally wed after everything they've been through."

"Then we'll go out and celebrate that too," Vorana said. "No more objections. I'll get the hatchling settled while you grab your coats and shoes. Meet you outside in five minutes."

"I'll come with you to settle the baby," I said. "She's sad because Finn is no longer around."

"I'll come too," Sage said. "I don't trust that little fire-breather. Her flame burns hotter every day."

The three of us, and the hatchling, who was more than happy to be carried by Vorana despite her size, headed into the backyard, while Sorcha and Zandra cleared the table of our barely touched meal. It wouldn't go to waste. We'd eat it later for supper.

The baby whimpered when Vorana settled her in her flameproof bed, which had pictures of rabbits on it, so I hopped in with her to lull her for a while and offer my ears as comforter suckers. Well, I say suckers. Now the hatchling had teeth, she chewed. However, I accepted the discomfort, because I knew she found solace when gnawing on my ears.

"Watch out for her," Sage grumbled. "A burp in the wrong direction, and you'll be toast."

"She's getting better at controlling her flame," Vorana said, "but she needs a dragon guide. Someone who can teach her how to use it. Finn did his best, and I'm doing what I can. I've learned so much about how to look after a dragon since she arrived, but she needs her own family around her."

"Finn asked us to look after her," I said. "But I gently suggested the same thing."

"We're not fostering her," Sage said. "She's way too dangerous. I know she doesn't mean it when she blasts out flames when she gets excited, but she'll incinerate us with an errant belch. And I get that she's cute, but she's also deadly. We can't have an untrained deadly creature roaming around town. She's getting bigger all the time. Soon enough, she'll outgrow this place. Then what do we do with her?"

"I know," Vorana said. "I'll be sad to let her go, but it is for the best. And Finn will realize that too. He got in way over his head with this scaled sweetie."

"He's in way over his head with all of this," I said. "I still can't figure out what happened. Why would Finn murder his father when they'd just reunited?

And how did he get knocked out at the murder scene?"

"Demon power," Vorana said. "When it takes over, it takes a lot out of Finn. And when his angel and demon energy conflict, it's tiring for him."

"And he's taken on too much recently," Sage said. "The guy's not been taking care of himself. He gets tired, and things fall apart in a fiery mess of murder."

I huffed out my unhappiness, dissatisfied with both responses.

Five minutes later, the hatchling was asleep, and I gently extracted my ear from her mouth. Vorana kindly healed the bite marks, and then we were on our way with the others, heading toward the bar. I felt no more cheerful, but I didn't want to let everyone else down.

We walked along in companionable silence, although Vorana, Sorcha, and Zandra occasionally made comments about the upcoming wedding.

Sage trundled beside me in her harness. "Focus on your witch, not Finn. Look at the good stuff in your life."

I glanced at her. "It's not like you to be so upbeat."

"Yeah, I've been hanging around with some annoyingly positive types who have been influencing me."

I chuffed out a laugh. "I need to fix up Zandra and Randal. Neither of them has made a move to ask the other to the wedding."

"Those two are terrible at progressing their relationship," Sage said. "They should stick to being friends."

"When there's so much possibility between them?" I shook my head. "Do you know anything about the person Torrin's been dating?"

"News to me. When you told us he was having woman trouble, I wasn't surprised. He used to run wild when he was younger. But this is the first I've heard about him getting serious with anyone."

I slowed as we reached Torrin's repair store. It was already closed. "I thought he stayed open late."

"He runs the place, so I guess he can open and shut whenever he likes," Sage said. "Shall we get ribs at the bar? I've finally got my appetite back."

"Ribs? With your lack of teeth?"

"I can suck them!" She gave me a playful paw thump.

I remained staring at Torrin's closed repair store. It had been shut the last time I'd passed by. In fact, I couldn't remember the last time I'd seen him working.

"He's probably already in the bar drowning his sorrows," Sage said, already following the others. "You can talk to him about his woman trouble over a plate of barbecue glazed ribs."

I let them go ahead and sniffed around Torrin's shop. There was a faint whiff of sulfur, but he was part dragon, so that was no surprise. I sat back and took a moment to look around. Things felt wrong. It was as if a part of Crimson Cove was falling apart. I might have my glorious fur back and Sammy by my side, but I was unhappy. And I wouldn't be happy until I got Finn out of trouble.

"Juno!" Zandra waved me over to the bar. "Sage wants ribs. Shall I get some for you, too?"

I headed into the bar with her. "No ribs for me."

"Where are you going?" Zandra asked.

"To find Torrin."

"Suit yourself. We're grabbing a booth at the back. Bring Torrin over when you find him."

It took me ten minutes to do a slow circuit of the bar. Torrin wasn't there. And after checking with the bartender, he hadn't been in for days. No one had seen him, and no one knew where he was. It was something else to add to the worrying list of things I was unhappy about.

What was going on in Crimson Cove? Whatever it was, a pitcher of margarita and some sticky ribs wouldn't solve it.

I pressed my cold booping snooter against Zandra's cheek, and she flinched. I huffed into her ear and gently batted her face to wake her.

"What is it?" she muttered, still half-asleep.

"I have an idea," I whispered.

"Come back in a couple of hours. It's too early."

"This is important." I booped her cheek again.

"I need more sleep. I had one too many of those fruity cocktails last night. Vorana is a terrible influence."

"She does enjoy her cocktails," I said. "This is about Finn. More precisely, the flames that killed Doyle."

Zandra puffed out a breath and opened her eyes. She blinked several times. "Go on."

"I contacted Bell Blackthorn and Hodgepodge." We'd met Bell and her wyvern familiar Hodgepodge during a recent investigation into Cythera's near miss with poison from a dragon bottle.

"Why would you do that?"

"Because they're dragon experts. We're meeting them in an hour."

Zandra turned her head and stared at me. "I still don't get it. Why do you think they know something about Finn?"

"I've been awake all night going over things. We know it's hard to kill a demon, but one thing that's guaranteed to mortally wound them is another demon's flame. It's super hot and powerful."

"Exactly. Which is how Doyle was killed."

"Or was he? Think about it. The only thing that burns as hot as demon flame is dragon fire."

Zandra sucked in a breath. "I'm definitely listening now."

I danced from paw to paw. "What if a dragon set Finn up? They've been lurking around Crimson Cove for a while. They know someone in this town is hiding a dragon hatchling. And they were getting close to Finn. A dragon burned down one of his barns. Then we caught that fake wedding celebrant skulking around at the sanctuary, trying to find the hatchling. He said he'd told his friends about Finn and his secret. He must have meant our dragon baby."

"You think a dragon wants Finn to suffer because he kept the egg?" Zandra sat up and rubbed her forehead. "Don't answer. I need coffee to process this. Let's go up to the kitchen."

"Get dressed first. We don't have long. Bell starts work just after dawn, but when I expressed how urgent this matter was, she agreed to meet us as soon as possible."

"I still need my coffee," Zandra said.

"Take it to go."

Ten minutes later, Zandra was dressed, thermos mug in hand, and we were on our way to meet Bell and Hodgepodge. A flicker of orange slid the day into view as we hurried along the silent streets.

I rode on Zandra's shoulder, wrapped around her neck to keep out the early morning chill.

"I'm not dismissing your theory, but it's a long shot," Zandra said. "Don't get your hopes up and think this will get Finn free."

"Of course, my hopes are up! This makes total sense. Finn pushed his luck for too long, and the dragons have retaliated. They framed him for murder, took away his father, and stole his freedom because they want their hatchling back, and they want to punish him, too."

"And you think Bell and Hodgepodge will know about this dragon plot to ruin Finn?"

"No, but they know their dragons. They live in a realm that was once jointly ruled by dragons. They can get us to the right person, or rather, the right dragon, so we can find out what they know about Finn."

"I'm not sure I want to tangle with dragons," Zandra said. "We've got enough problems."

"We have no problems, other than that one of our best friends is behind bars. We'll get him free. I know this will work." I urged Zandra on to the meeting place. Bell said they'd use their impressive tunnel portal system to get to Crimson Cove for our meeting, and then they'd take us to an as-yet-undisclosed location.

We hurried along the quiet wooded pathway through Crimson Cove woods then diverted off the path through the undergrowth until we reached a stone wall. Although it looked solid, I knew better, having experienced the incredible system Bell and Hodgepodge used to get around. According to Bell, the system had been created by dragons a long time ago, but not everyone could use it.

Zandra tugged her jacket tighter around herself and sipped on her coffee as we waited in the chilly silence.

I licked one of her unruly eyebrows into place. "You need to look your best."

"For what? Bell doesn't strike me as fashion-conscious."

"I have a feeling we're about to meet some impressive creatures. Bell and Hodgepodge claim to be lowly servants, but they have an affinity with dragons."

Zandra opened her mouth to ask more questions, but stone grated together, and a few seconds later, a hole appeared in the solid rock. Bell poked her head out and smiled. Hodgepodge was draped around her neck just like I was on Zandra's. Bell was an attractive forty-something with dark hair and large dark eyes. Hodgepodge was a handsome mottled brown with a long, fat tail.

Bell lifted a pale hand in greeting. "Hey! We got here as soon as we could. I hope you haven't been waiting long."

Zandra shook her head. "A couple of minutes. Sorry for dragging you away at such short notice. I didn't know Juno was planning this."

"We shouldn't be doing this." Hodgepodge scowled at me. "Too risky."

"We had to help." Bell rested a hand against his side. "Finn's a nice guy. And he's far too pretty to go behind bars." A faint flush flooded her cheeks. "How's he doing?"

"He's been better," I said. "We appreciate your help in solving this mystery."

"It's dangerous, poking about in dragon business," Hodgepodge said. "And there's no proof dragons were involved in killing your demon. Your dumb angel laddie could have lost control and done the fiery deed."

"Hodgie, if an innocent angel is behind bars, we must help him get free. It's the right thing to do," Bell said.

"What if it gets us in trouble? And you can't be late getting to work. The dragons need us."

"Hodgepodge is right," Bell said on a sigh. "We have little time, but we'll help."

"I'm still out of the loop here," Zandra said. "What don't we have much time for?"

Bell grinned, excitement lighting her face. "We have no dragons in our own realm, but I'm taking you to Wild Wing."

Zandra shrugged. "And what's Wild Wing?"

Bell's smile deepened. "It's a dragon haven. Some even call it paradise. Want to meet some incredible dragons?"

Chapter 20

Enter the dragon

"Is Wild Wing safe?" I was perched on Zandra's shoulder as we dashed after Bell and Hodgepodge, along the stone corridor.

"It's neutral ground for dragons and anyone who enjoys their company," Bell said. "But you must be respectful and follow their rules. It's the only way they can ensure order. They don't tolerate any breaches." She stopped by another stone wall and placed a hand against it. There was a faint glow from underneath her palm, and another door appeared. "This will take us there. And I must urge you to hurry."

"We'll be as quick as we can," Zandra said. "Juno set this up, so she's taking the lead."

"I'm sure I'm onto something," I said. "But I need to speak to a dragon to be certain."

"Get ready to meet more than a few," Bell said. "Wild Wing is full of them. But I've arranged for us to meet Willow. She's from the Mako Realm. They used to be closely allied with the Ithric dragons before they died out."

"Bell took a great risk reaching out to Willow," Hodgepodge said. "I told her not to do it. We don't enjoy brushing up against danger."

"No one does, but your help is appreciated," I said. "And I'm certain Finn will thank you personally once he's been released."

Bell ducked her head. "There's no need for that, but it'll be nice to see him again. This way. Stay close. The seal on my wrist ensures your safety, but the protective power only stretches so far."

The stone corridor was narrow and smelled damp as we walked along it. It swiftly opened up, and we stepped out into a lush forest. The path, soft underfoot and lined with luminous flowers, wound through towering trees. The air was alive with the gentle rustling of leaves and the delicate trills of songbirds, accompanied by the occasional deep resonant hum of a dragon's purr. From the canopy above, colorful creatures with huge wings fluttered by, each one radiating a soft glow, illuminating the forest like living lanterns.

My gaze lifted as dragons of all sizes and colors soared through the sky. They looped and twirled, their scales shimmering in the shifting light. The deep-throated calls of dragons echoed through the woods, vibrating in my bones.

Bell stood to one side, Hodgepodge still wrapped around her neck, a knowing smile on her face. "I figured you'd want a minute to take it all in. It's something else, isn't it?"

"I've heard of dragon havens," I said, "but I've never visited one. It's extraordinary."

"I haven't been here in a while." Bell's tone was wistful. "Work at the castle keeps me busy, and when I get a day off, I spend it cozied up in bed reading a book or napping with Hodgie."

"Best thing to do," Hodgepodge said. "Stay inside where you won't get noticed."

"We're being noticed now." The note of concern in Zandra's voice had my hackles lifting. I focused on a petite red and black striped dragon who studied us from across the field.

"Don't worry. That's Willow. I let her know we were coming," Bell said. "Do you know how to greet a dragon?"

"Three bows from the waist then extending the hand. Since I have neither a waist nor a hand, I'll bow as low as I can and extend my paw," I said.

"How do you know that?" Zandra murmured.

"I've met dragons. They're a fiercely intelligent species, but they love their old-fashioned rules."

"Nothing wrong with a bit of good old-fashioned courtesy," Hodgepodge said.

"Are you ready to meet Willow?" Bell asked. "She can be sharp, but she has a pure heart."

"We're ready," Zandra said. "What does Willow know about the situation we're dealing with?"

"Bell and Hodgepodge know it's Finn in trouble, who the other suspects are, and what happened to Doyle," I said. "We shouldn't use names or locations when talking to Willow. I... I also mentioned the dragon egg."

Zandra shot me a surprised glance. We knew it wouldn't be long before we had to return the hatchling, so I figured we might as well start the groundwork and hope to avoid any serious conflict with the dragons.

Bell nodded as she guided us along the path toward Willow. "Willow knows you're looking for answers to help an angel hybrid accused of murder and about the abandoned dragon egg. That's the reason she so swiftly agreed to this meeting. Dragons only produce one egg every five years, so they're fiercely protective of all infants."

We stopped a respectful distance from Willow. I hopped off Zandra's shoulder, and we started our formal greetings. All of us bowed to Willow three times and then extended either our hands, paws, or clawed feet.

Willow lowered herself to the ground, resting her scaled chin on the grass. "Welcome to Wild Wing." Her voice was a tuneful, deep melody, softer than I'd expected. "Bell Blackthorn, Hodgepodge. It has been too long."

"Apologies." Bell straightened, and so did we. "My work at the castle is never-ending. Everyone wants to see the stone dragons and leave their offerings."

Willow's black eyes narrowed a fraction. "My heart still hurts when I remember what happened in your realm. Such a tragedy and a mystery. If your castle guardians weren't so secretive, we would assist them in uncovering what happened to Emberthorn and his companions. But they have ignored all offers of bonds and friendship."

"They're most likely licking their wounds after their failure," Hodgepodge muttered.

"We still seek an audience with them," Willow said. "We must learn how the alliance broke down so swiftly. And I hear your realm suffers."

"We've not had many happy times since the dragons left," Bell said, glancing at us.

Willow turned her attention toward Zandra and me. "Of course. It's a pleasure to meet you both. I trust Bell and Hodgepodge have explained how Wild Wing works."

I nodded. "We'll be respectful. But we seek answers to a troubling problem."

"I've heard the basics from my friends. An angel is accused of murder?"

"That's right. He's an angel hybrid."

"I understand he's both demon and angel. That's an unusual combination. They don't usually get along. Well, not long enough to create a child."

"This angel hybrid is unique. Good and kind. He'd never commit murder," I said.

"You doubt the word of the eyewitness?" Willow asked.

"He's credible, but I believe there's more to this mystery," I said. "As we all know, demons are hard to kill. Only magical flame from another demon, beheading, a few deadly spells, or dragon fire destroys them. And it's dragon fire we're most interested in as the cause of death."

Smoke emerged from Willow's nostrils. "You believe a dragon murdered this demon and left your angel friend to take the blame? We don't interfere in other magical creatures' activities. We're busy looking after our own realms and people. It serves no purpose for us to meddle with others."

Zandra shifted beside me. "Hypothetically speaking, if someone found a dragon egg and didn't return it to you, what would happen to them?"

Willow rose, and a growl rumbled in her chest. "No one would be so foolish as to do such a thing. There are legends, of course, of so-called heroic knights sent on quests to retrieve dragon eggs in the ridiculous belief it would grant them long life, untold riches, and power. We're always happy to squash those myths. Our eggs aren't trinkets to be used by others."

"If an egg was part of this murder investigation, would it prompt a dragon to become involved?" I asked.

Willow was silent for several seconds. "Is that the case?"

"We're thinking of all the reasons a dragon may framc our friend for murder," I said. "If he took something of yours that was valuable, and I'm not saying he did, would you punish him?"

"Anyone who interferes with our hatchlings is strongly punished. Do I need to be concerned about this angel?" Willow addressed the question to Bell and Hodgepodge.

"I've met him," Bell said. "Juno's description is accurate. He has a good heart, and he healed Hodgepodge when he wandered off and got himself injured."

"Bell also considers him extremely handsome," Hodgepodge muttered.

"What angel isn't?" Willow bared her teeth in what I assumed was a dragon smile. "I trust your judgments, so I'll make no harsh assumptions about this angel. But if he did something extremely unwise and took a precious thing that belongs to us, he'll be in a lot of trouble."

"Enough trouble that you'd consider framing him for murder so he loses everything?" I asked.

More smoke drifted from Willow's nose. "We wouldn't frame him for murder."

"What would you do to him?" Zandra asked.

"It's possible he'd be tracked and intimidated, encouraged to do the right thing. If that failed, he'd be brought before a tribunal with the angels and the dragons deciding his fate." Willow lowered herself back to the ground. "We don't go around murdering people, though. It is not our way. We're a peace-loving species. We live in harmony with all, although some make it less easy than others."

"What about if a mother lost her egg?" I asked. "Again, hypothetically speaking, perhaps she fell into a rage and was unable to control herself. She learned someone had her baby and acted on instinct to protect it."

"We have protocols dragons follow, whether they're part of a realm or live independently. Anyone who breaks the rules is punished."

"But it is possible?"

Willow was quiet for a long time. "When we suffer loss, we go into a swift decline, and our bodies shut down. When a mother loses her infant, she can barely function. If this hypothetical mother lost her hatchling before it was born, she'd have fallen into a deep hibernation to protect her heart from shattering because of grief. She'd have been unable to plan a complicated ruse to murder someone and frame another for it."

The hope I'd carried inside me died. The more we spoke to Willow, the less likely it seemed that dragon flame ended Doyle's life.

"I see this information hasn't brought you happiness," Willow said. "But I'm most interested in talking to you more about this hypothetical taken egg scenario. Especially since there have been rumors about a missing dragon egg."

"We should stick to facts, not wild rumors," I said.

"You understand I need to push you on this," Willow said. "You'd do the same if your kittens went missing."

"True. But there's little we can tell you." Or rather, very little we were willing to tell. And if Finn really was going to prison for murdering Doyle, that would be punishment enough, and we'd have no option but to return the hatchling to the dragons. And from what I was learning about Willow, they'd take the greatest care of her.

Willow considered my answer. "If time allows, permit me to show you around Wild Wing. It's a peaceful place where all are welcome, as long as you respect our harmony. Perhaps when you get to know me better, you'll become more open with your knowledge."

"We've got a little time before we have to return to the castle," Bell said. "I'd love to see what's changed since our last visit."

"Then follow me." Willow turned and ambled away, her movements graceful despite her size. She may be a petite dragon, but she was still suitably impressive.

We walked along a beautiful tree-lined avenue, leaves holding their first tinge of orange as the heat of summer gave way to cooler months.

"We have a number of smaller villages here. Anyone who visits can stay in any of them, and they provide different types of entertainment. There's a space for people who enjoy music, those who enjoy dance, and those who prefer silence. We cater to everybody," Willow said. "In each village, the streets are wide and cobblestoned, allowing dragons and larger magical beings to traverse easily. The buildings have also been designed to harmonize with the natural environment, often incorporating living elements such as trees, flowers, and vines, where dragons and other creatures find sanctuary and community."

"It sounds great." Zandra looked around as we reached the first row of houses.

"This is Stardust Hollow. See the dragon-sized perches? They're made from ancient forest trees that had fallen," Willow said. "I imagine they'd be suitable for sharpening claws if you're interested, Juno."

I admired the mighty branches, many scattered with plush cushions to make for a comfy resting spot. Wild Wing was growing on me.

"We also have Crystal Cascade. The homes are carved into the sides of the cliffs, and the waterfall is a popular bathing spot. The Ethereal Glade is full of healing flowers and herbs, which is ideal for those who need to rest and recover." Willow lifted a scaled foot toward the horizon. "And Ember Ridge is nestled near a dormant volcano. Dragons adore the warmth."Top of Form

As we explored, we had the place almost to ourselves, and there were only a few individuals dressed in long, plain robes hurrying around as the morning stirred to life.

I watched one of the robed men pass by, carrying an armful of rolled papers. He disappeared into a building and then came out a few moments later. He was dressed differently from the last time I'd seen him, less seasoned camper and more monkish assistant, but I instantly recognized Rembrandt Flicker.

"Juno, keep up," Zandra said. "Willow is going to show us the distillery. They have honey mead and seed cake."

I gestured for her to come over, and she hurried back to me. "Look who's here."

She squinted at the man as he returned with another armful of paper scrolls. "Is that the camping guy we questioned? Rembrandt?"

I nodded. "The eyewitness who watched Finn kill Doyle. What's he doing here? He said he was going home after he'd finished camping."

By this time, Willow, Bell, and Hodgepodge had turned and were walking back toward us to see what had caught our attention.

"Is something wrong?" Willow asked.

"Who's that man?" I asked.

"That's René Seax. He's one of my most trusted and loyal aides. He's been with me for over three hundred years."

"He's looking good on it," Zandra said.

"Dragon aides are gifted some of our power and extra-long lives as a reward for their service."

"Loyalty and rewards for good service," I murmured, more to myself than anyone else.

Willow nodded. "It's only right. Aides give up everything to spend their lives with us. Why the interest in him?"

"Because René has been lying to us."

Chapter 21

A twist in the tale

I dashed away, ignoring calls from the others, and followed René into a building. I stood by the entrance, waiting as he set down more scrolls. He was muttering to himself under his breath. When he turned to the door, he didn't see me straight away. It was only when he was almost on top of me that his gaze drifted down, and his eyes widened in stark recognition.

"Greetings, Rembrandt. Or should I say, René? Did you change your travel plans after we met in Crimson Cove?"

His mouth flapped open and closed. He took several steps back then launched himself over my head, hitting the ground outside and rolling to his feet.

"Oh, no you don't. You have questions to answer." I chased after him. "Why did you give us a false name?"

René didn't slow and sped away from me, his arms and legs pumping.

"Juno! Wait," Zandra yelled.

"I've almost caught him." I kept my focus on René, briefly slowing to ensure Zandra caught up. "He must be behind all of this!"

Zandra wheezed out a breath as she joined me, and we raced after René. "But why? Do you think Willow ordered him to frame Finn?"

"I sense only goodness in Willow. But if René is loyal to her, and he overheard her talking about a missing dragon egg, he could have started his own investigation."

"And he wanted to make Willow proud by catching the person and ruining them. Oh, boy. This is one big old mess we need to fix."

"We've got him!"

René had turned down a dead end. He stopped by a stone wall and turned to face us.

"You're coming with us." I stalked toward him, my fur fluffed. "The eyewitness account about Finn killing Doyle was a lie, wasn't it?"

He held out his hands, panic in his gaze. "You can't do this. Not here. Wild Wing is a sacred place. I'm protected."

"We'll do anything we have to do to ensure our friend doesn't spend the rest of his life behind bars. You're returning to Crimson Cove and telling the truth."

"I did nothing wrong. I'll always protect my dragons. You made a mistake by coming here." René blasted out a fiery spell that swept around us.

We dove to the side, narrowly avoiding the searing heat. I leaped into action, furious at his attempt to harm my witch. Zandra threw out a shield spell around us as we stalked toward René.

He chanted an incantation, summoning hot shadows that twisted and coiled around him like serpents. The darkness surged toward us, and I bared my teeth, muscles tensed as I crouched low.

Zandra's magic surged forward, knocking René to the ground.

Flames burst forth from his fingertips, flames that hungered for destruction. But my water spell met the fiery onslaught head-on, extinguishing the fire with a satisfying hiss.

I soared through the air, murder mittens primed to pin him. But René was no pushover, and with a flick of his wrist, he sent a burst of hot energy hurtling my way. I twisted in mid-air, trying to avoid the collision, but the impact sent me into a wall.

"Juno!" Zandra's voice was a mixture of worry and anger.

"I'm unhurt." Pushing through the pain, I sprang onto my paws. Zandra and I exchanged a determined glance, our unspoken agreement echoing between us. It was time to bring René down and make him sorry for messing with Finn.

He summoned a ring of flames around him, making me hunch away from the heat.

"How much dragon fire does this guy have?" Concern flickered through Zandra's words. "He keeps getting hotter."

"We can beat him. He's not getting away with framing Finn."

Shouts and dragon growls drew my attention. Our fight had been noticed. I launched myself at René once more. He raised his hands, attempting to repel me with a burst of magic, but I was quicker. My murder mittens connected with his arm, leaving deep gashes. René roared in pain and anger, his power waning as blood seeped from the wounds.

Zandra's magic swirled around us, and René staggered, his defenses shattering.

With a surge of magical energy, my jaws closed around René's wrist, pinning his hand to the ground. His eyes widened in shock as I held him in place, his dragon magic flickering like dying embers.

A painfully tight grip wrapped around my middle, and I was lifted into the air. Willow had hold of me in her claws, and she wasn't alone. Two more angry dragons were with her, and one of them held Zandra.

I blasted out my rage, furious that they were holding Zandra against her will. "Let me go."

"You've broken countless laws by fighting," Willow's voice boomed out. "This unforgivable behavior must be punished."

"You don't understand. It's René!" Willow's claws wrapped around my head, preventing me from speaking.

"I'm so angry I could crush you. There is no fighting in Wild Wing. It is our first rule and is always upheld."

I cared nothing for that rule as I kicked and squirmed in her bone-crushing grasp, desperate to get to Zandra and determined to stop René from getting away.

I conjured a spell and blasted it out. For a second, I was free from the dragon's grip, but she swooped down and caught me. During my tumble, I spotted Bell and Hodgepodge running beneath us. I found myself upside down, my front paws dangling freely. Another dragon was sailing along beside us, Zandra still in its claws. She looked unconscious.

I screeched my rage and fought against Willow, but she snarled and tightened her grip so much I almost passed out.

"You're lucky to still be alive," Willow said. "If you didn't have Bell and Hodgepodge's friendship, you'd be dead, and so would your witch."

Before I could utter a word, she swooped low and released me from her hold. I plunged through the air, into a hole in the ground, and landed on a damp straw floor. I rolled over and jumped, but the hole had already been covered, leaving the pit with only gloomy, gray light.

I threw a release spell at the ceiling. It ricocheted back, slammed into the walls several times, and then hit me, knocking me off my paws and rolling me over several times. I grunted as my own magic worked against me and sparked through my fur, pinching, nipping, and stinging my skin.

After taking a few seconds to recover, I was on my paws again, searching for an escape. There had to be a way out. They couldn't separate me from Zandra. And I had to get back to René. He was a loyal dragon aide, and he must have thought he was doing the right thing by framing Finn. Or maybe I'd gotten Willow wrong, and she was behind this. She'd ordered her aide to find out what had happened to the missing egg and punish whoever had it. Whatever the reason, I'd be no good to anyone while I was stuck in here.

I dashed around the pit, searching for a weakness, a way out. But the only way in was the sealed hole above my head. I growled and spat and scratched the walls with my murder mittens, feeling furiously impatient. I tugged hard on the bond I had with Zandra and was relieved to feel it was still there. She may be unconscious, but she was alive.

I conjured another release spell but held it between my paws. There must be dragon magic surrounding this prison. If I used another spell, the power would only return to injure me. I extinguished the spell and slumped onto my belly. I'd find a way out, and I would get back to my witch. I'd fight a hundred dragons if I had to, but no one would separate us.

"Glad to see you've come to your senses," a low male voice grumbled from the shadows.

I was back on my paws, my hackles raised. "Who's there? Show yourself."

"I would, but I can barely move. Dragon shackles are something else. They sting like an angry thornspire pixie when you try to get out of them."

I tilted my head. That voice was familiar. It was rough around the edges, but I recognized it. I crept closer to where the sound had come from, my eyes slowly adjusting to the dimness. I stopped as I was met with a set of metal bars preventing me from going any farther.

"You keep throwing out spells like that, and you'll kill yourself. I tried it several times before I knocked myself out. When I woke, I was in enchanted chains."

The more the man spoke, the more I was certain I knew who this was. I inhaled deeply and got a hit of a familiar musky sulfur scent, which confirmed what I already knew. "Torrin, is that you?"

Chapter 22

Another twist

Torrin Connor's grimy face appeared behind the bars, his eyes wide in disbelief. "Juno! How are you here?"

"I could ask you the same thing. I noticed your repair shop closed, and no one has seen you for days, but I didn't expect to find you in a dragon pit. How long have you been here?"

He swiped a hand down his face. "I've lost track of time. Three days? Maybe more."

"Why do they have you held captive?"

"Long story. I... I got myself into a mess," he said.

"Does this have to do with the woman you're dating?"

"How do you know about her?"

"That's also a long story. And since there's no way out of here, we should share."

Torrin's eyebrows flashed up. "You first. How did you get into Wild Wing? There's not exactly an open invitation to come hang with the dragons."

"I'm here with Zandra. We have connections in the Ithric realm."

"The place that doesn't have dragons anymore?" He shook his head. "I still don't follow."

"That's how we got our invitation. Zandra and I think Finn's been set up by someone who works with the dragons." I wrinkled my booping snooter. Torrin smelled disgusting, and there was dried blood on his ripped shirt.

"Set up how?"

"He's been framed for murdering his father."

Torrin's forehead wrinkled. "That's impossible."

"We know! But the evidence against him is overwhelming. At least, it was until I discovered the so-called credible eyewitness is unreliable and working as a dragon aide right here in Wild Wing."

Torrin took a few seconds to process the information and then shook his head again. "No, I mean, it would have been impossible for Finn to murder his dad. He's already dead."

It was my turn to show surprise. "You knew Finn's father?"

He leaned back against the wall and slid down it. "Yeah, although I never told Finn about this. I learned a while back that his biological dad was killed. He was a proper scumbag. I met him when I was doing business out of town. He was drunk and bragging about how incredible his life was. Then he talked about how one of his many offspring joined Angel Force after they opened the doors to misfits, his word, not mine. He was going on about how he'd get away with any crime since he had a son on the inside. At first, I didn't pay him any attention, but then he said Finn's name."

"Did you confront him?"

"No, but I kept an eye on him. I wanted to make sure he didn't rock up in Crimson Cove and exploit Finn. One day, I got news he'd been killed in a bar fight. No loss."

"So, the demon who came to Crimson Cove claiming to be Finn's father was an impostor," I said. "I had my doubts about him."

"Whoever that guy was, he wasn't Finn's dad."

"You never told Finn you met his real dad?"

"I thought about it, but I figured it wouldn't do him any good. Finn doesn't often talk about his childhood, but I knew it was rough. And he never once mentioned he wanted to find his biological family, so I left it in the past. There wouldn't have been a good outcome if they'd met. And since that loser got himself in trouble, I decided not to stir things."

"The impostor, Doyle, must have wanted to get into Finn's life for some reason," I said. "He didn't come to Crimson Cove alone. He brought friends. They must have been in on the deception, too."

"Maybe he was fooling them all," Torrin said. "Demons. Never trust them."

"It's something to investigate once I get out of here," I said. "What about you? Why are the dragons holding you?"

"I'll answer that in a second. Why did you get tossed in here?"

"The eyewitness! The one who claimed to see Finn murder his father. He set this up. We came to Wild Wing because I had an idea a dragon framed Finn because he's concealing something that belongs to them."

Torrin grimaced. "You mean the hatchling?"

I settled on the damp straw. "I wondered if you knew about her."

He shrugged. "Finn asked for some advice, but I don't know how to rear an infant dragon. I tried to help by teaching her a few flame tricks, but I'm not sure how useful I was. You think the dragons are onto Finn?"

"I guarantee they are."

Torrin whistled low. "And you think this eyewitness was sent to frame him?"

"That's why I'm in here. I saw René and chased him. Willow, the dragon we've been speaking to, didn't appreciate me breaking their laws, so she tossed me in here. They took Zandra, too. I must get back to her."

"That's some serious trouble you've gotten yourself into. You don't mess around in this place. You can't bend the rules when you've got ridiculously powerful supernatural creatures stomping around and blasting out flames." Torrin blew out a breath. "I don't know how you're getting yourself out of this."

"I will. And I'll be reunited with Zandra. So, your story."

Torrin shrugged. "You guessed right. I'm in here because of a woman. The woman I'm madly in love with. The woman I'd die for."

"The dragons don't approve of your union?"

He scratched his forehead. "That's where things get tricky. You see, she's from an influential dragon shifter community. We're basically talking princess-level. I didn't know that when we met. She was just a cool lady with a great sense of humor and an incredible..." He gestured at his chest.

"Go on. You started dating, and her community didn't approve?"

"They hated it. She reassured me they'd come around and even introduced me to her family. The next thing I know, I'm getting veiled threats. Then my repair shop gets broken into and a not-so-sweet note shoved through the door warning me what'll happen if I don't stop dating her. Of course, I ignored it."

"And ended up in here. That's illegal," I said.

"Tell that to the angry dragon shifters. I'm like Finn, a misfit, too. Her family may not have had a problem with us fooling around, but I asked her to marry me, and she said yes." Torrin gave me a huge, goofy smile. "The second word got back to her family that we were engaged, it was like I'd lit a match to an explosive. They wasted no time in taking her and ensuring I ended up here. Like I said, they have royal blood and lots of power."

"You can't keep true love from prevailing," I said.

A wry smile crossed his face. "You sound like Madeleine. She said true love would win against anything. She sounded so certain, and she repeated it so many times, I believed her. But love against a family of angry dragon shifters who have power and influence? Not a chance. After they convinced the dragons to lock me up, I got a dose of cold, hard reality."

"Love wins over everything," I said. "We'll beat this. And we are getting out. We have to. I need to reunite with Zandra. You need to be with Madeline, and I'm determined to confront René to ensure Finn's freedom."

"I'm with you, Juno," Torrin said. "But there's only one way in and out. I've searched every inch of this place, and it's secure. And as you found out for yourself, they don't mess around with the magic wards."

"If we can't get out, Zandra will rescue us. She's close by, and our bond is strong."

A grating sound overhead had me tensing.

"Be careful," Torrin whispered. "They might be throwing someone else in or taking us out."

Hodgepodge's head appeared in the opening. "Get over here, you wee fluffy idiot. The dragons want to speak to you."

I dashed over. "Torrin, too?"

"I know nothing about a Torrin."

"He's a friend. The dragons have him held against his will on a false charge."

"Don't worry about me," Torrin said. "This is your chance. You won't get another."

"Bell has spoken for you, so the dragons will listen. I can't do anything for your friend there," Hodgepodge said.

"Get yourself free," Torrin said.

"I won't forget you're in here," I said. "I'll make the dragons see reason."

"Good luck with that," he said.

I wasted no time and threw myself into the air, using a little extra magic to bounce and get through the hole. Hodgepodge caught hold of me with his tail to steady me as I landed.

He hissed at me and shook his head. "You're lucky Bell is so kind-hearted. I told her not to get involved and this would only bring trouble to our door, but she can never ignore someone in need of help."

"For that, she has my eternal gratitude," I said. "Where's Zandra?"

"Bell got her out. They've been talking with Willow and the other dragons to calm things down and ensure total destruction doesn't take place. You'll need to do serious groveling to Willow to get out of Wild Wing alive." Hodgepodge thumped my head with his heavy tail. "No fighting! It's a simple rule, yet you smashed into it the second you were let loose. Ya wee bampot."

I had to assume a bampot wasn't a term of fondness. "I broke the rules for a good reason."

"Lucky for you, Willow's interested enough to hear those reasons. But I should warn you, the assistant you chased has been with Willow for hundreds of years, and she's never had reason to doubt him. If you're basing this on a hunch—"

"I'm not! And why would René run if he had nothing to hide?"

"That's one of the arguments Bell and Zandra used. Willow is an ancient dragon, and she's seen it all. So long as you're level-headed and don't go in all spells blazing, you'll get a fair hearing."

"Thanks, Hodgepodge."

"Don't thank me. I told Bell this was a mistake. This way."

We only had to travel a short distance before we came to a vast, open cobbled space. Willow stood at one end with two large green dragons flanking her. There were a number of dragon aides all dressed in robes, and standing in front of the dragons were Bell and Zandra. As soon as Zandra saw me, she broke away from the group and ran toward me.

I flung myself into her arms, curling around her neck several times before finally resting my forehead against hers and spending a few seconds breathing in her deliciously familiar scent.

"Did they hurt you?" I whispered.

"No, although I don't ever want to ride in a dragon's claws again. It's worse than the Big Dipper. My stomach is churning. You?"

"I'm good. But when they threw me into the pit, I wasn't alone."

"What was down there with you?"

"Torrin Conner! The dragons have him imprisoned because he's dating a dragon shapeshifter. Once we deal with this situation, we need to get him free."

Zandra drew back her head, her eyes wide. "One problem at a time, yeah?"

I nodded, and we walked over with Hodgepodge to join Willow and Bell. We went through the formal bow greeting again, then I looked up at Willow. She regarded me with a cold calmness.

"I hope you value the strong friendships you have made," Willow said. "Bell has spoken for you, and I'm prepared to listen to what you have to say."

I nodded my appreciation at Bell, who remained silent. "Forgive me for breaking the rules and chasing René. When I discovered he was here, I was surprised, and I reacted badly."

Willow nodded. "Anyone who comes to Wild Wing knows of the power that resides here. If the rules are broken, many could be harmed."

"I regret my actions. And I wouldn't have chased him, but he ran when I approached him."

"Which is why you and your companion have been given the opportunity to plead your case," Willow said. "Bring René out."

René shuffled over, his head down as two other dragon aides brought him in front of us. He glanced at me but swiftly looked away, a scowl on his face.

"You believe my aide had something to do with your imprisoned angel friend," Willow said.

I nodded. "When the murder happened, the evidence against the angel seemed indisputable. He'd been in a locked house with the victim. The victim was killed by what we believed to be demon flame. And there was a reliable eyewitness: René. However, when he spoke to Angel Force, he called himself Rembrandt Flicker and claimed to be on a wild camping trip that brought him to Crimson Cove. He said he passed by the house when the fight was happening and looked in the window to see the angel killing the demon."

A plume of smoke drifted from Willow's nostrils. "Was this angel the only suspect?"

I shook my head. "We focused on the victim's friends who traveled with him. They are all demons, so they have the power to kill him, but they have alibis. The evidence kept returning to the angel. But that angel's guilt was based only upon René's testimony."

Willow consulted with the two dragons on either side of her and then lowered her head to the ground and looked directly at René. "A dragon aide is incapable of lying to his dragon. René, what took you to Crimson Cove?"

His body shook, and he fell to his knees. "I did it for you!"

My breath caught in my throat. He was about to confess.

"What did you do?" Willow asked.

René hung his head. "There have been rumors about a stolen dragon egg. Then I overheard you talking to the others about your concerns. You said you wanted justice and for the baby to be returned. I heard from an outside contact that an infant dragon had been seen in Crimson Cove. So, I investigated."

"And what did you find?"

"A deceitful angel hybrid had stolen the egg. He was attempting to rear the hatchling as his own. I was convinced he'd corrupt the baby."

"Untrue," I said. "This angel is a good person. He made a mistake, a huge one, but he had no plans to do anything bad, and he had little control over his feelings for her."

Willow regarded me cooly. "You knew about this and kept it from me?"

"Not for any devious purpose," I said. "Someone left a dragon egg at an animal sanctuary. It was taken in by the angel and cared for. At the time, the egg was inactive, but after months of care, the baby woke and bonded with the angel. They love each other. She sang to him."

Willow's eyes widened. "It has been many years since I've heard of this, but it happens. So, the hatchling and the angel united?"

"Yes! The angel was doing his best to protect her, but it was a struggle, and he became concerned dragons were watching him."

"René, what did you do?" Willow stood and glared down at him. "Did you frame this angel for murder?"

René refused to look at her.

"Answer me. You cannot lie."

"But he can stay silent," Zandra murmured.

"Which only proves his guilt," I said.

Willow reached out a clawed foot. "Tell me the truth."

René hunched over. "I did it for you! You were concerned about the missing egg, so I found her. And she's so beautiful. A white dragon. Rare. I had to ensure the deceitful angel who'd captured her was punished."

Willow huffed out a smoky breath, while the dragons on either side of her growled. "You framed him for murder?"

"It was the right thing to do. Now, he's behind bars, and you know where the hatchling is. She's yours to take. You can bring her home."

Willow's enormous wings slumped. She talked quietly to her dragon companions for a moment before turning back to René. "You were given a rare and privileged gift when you became a dragon aide. Long life and incredible powers that must be respected."

"I respect them! And I used them for good. I used them to ensure we can get back our missing dragon."

"You used them for murder. You used your powers to frame an innocent angel who was doing his best. You know how strong a dragon bond is with any magical being if they don't have dragon blood in their veins. This angel would have had no way to free himself from the bonds the baby wrapped around him."

René looked shamefaced. "We had to get her back. And you said that action needed to be taken."

"You shouldn't have been listening to our private conversations," Willow said. "We were planning action but not murder. I'm bitterly disappointed in you."

"I did it for the right reasons."

Willow looked down at him, sadness in her eyes. "I release you from your role as my aide."

"No!" René fell to his knees. "Please, I'll do anything. I'm loyal to you. I did it for you."

Willow shook her head. "Our tie is broken. Once Angel Force has dealt with you, your powers will be removed." She looked at me. "You have our permission to take him away."

I bowed low. "We appreciate you listening and for helping us solve this mystery. But before we leave, we need to talk about the prisoner in your pit."

Chapter 23

Home and happiness

"I still can't believe that just over twenty-four hours ago, you and Zandra were in the middle of dragon territory, solving Finn's murder and getting Torrin free," Vorana said as she finished her makeup in the mirror in her bedroom.

Zandra lounged on the bed with me and Sage. She was wearing a pretty red dress and had even made an effort with her hair. She looked beautiful, but then she always did to me.

"I wonder how we get ourselves into these messes," Zandra said.

"I blame Juno," Sage said. "I prefer the quiet life."

I gently batted my friend with a velvet paw. "You'd get bored if I wasn't around to keep you entertained. And it worked out. René has been charged with Doyle's murder, and Finn is a free angel."

"How's Torrin?" Sorcha came into the room wearing a beautiful plum-colored dress, the hem resting on her knees.

"He was in pretty bad shape," I said, "but we were able to convince Willow and her companions to listen to his story. A dragon shapeshifter sold them a lie. They claimed Torrin abducted Madeline and held her prisoner. His fate was sealed until I discovered him in that pit."

"And they let him go just like that?" Sorcha gently adjusted the sparkling necklace she wore.

"It wasn't so simple," Zandra said. "Torrin was unable to keep his big mouth shut, which angered the dragons. But we contacted his girlfriend, and she confirmed everything. She'd gone willingly with Torrin, and they were in love. They planned to marry, but her family forcibly separated them and were keeping her imprisoned."

"Wow! You two never take the easy route, do you?" Vorana shook her head. "You were lucky to get out of there alive. I've heard about Wild Wing. It's a dangerous place."

"We may take the winding route to success, but we always get to where we need to be," I said. "Which is how we're here with all of you and about to witness two fine angels marry."

A knock came at the front door, so we all headed downstairs. Vorana opened the door to reveal Finn, Sorcha's date, Denver, and Randal Nix, looking handsome with a red bowtie that matched Zandra's dress.

She stared at him. "What are you doing here?"

He blushed and held out a corsage that matched her dress. "Being your wedding date, if that's okay. You said to pick you up from here, right?"

I stifled a laugh. Since neither of them had the courage to ask the other to the wedding, I'd set them up. And from the adorable flush on Zandra's face, it had been the perfect decision.

Zandra slid me a death stare then smiled at Randal. "Sure. I mean, I was planning to go with Juno, but..."

"No need to worry about me. My date's here," I said.

Sammy trotted along the pathway, his magnificent striped fur gleaming in the sunlight. We greeted each other with an affectionate rub of heads. I sat beside him as Sorcha's delectable date sweet-talked her before respectfully kissing her on the cheek.

Finn strolled over and crouched beside us. He wore a well-tailored soft gray suit with a white shirt underneath. "I thought I might accompany you, Juno, but I see my place has been taken."

"Regretfully so," I said, "but you're welcome to join us."

He grinned as he shook his head. "I'm good riding solo. But Sammy, if you could spare Juno for a moment, I need a word with her."

Sammy nodded. "Take good care of her."

"I always do." He led me away from the group. "We need to take a short flight."

"Where? We have to leave for the wedding soon," I said.

"Somewhere with plenty of space that's out of the way of prying eyes. Don't worry, we won't be late for the wedding. Cythera would fire me if I didn't show up. She's given me an important job."

"Fly slowly. Zandra took ages brushing my fur today, so it looks immaculate."

He laughed. "I'll make sure you don't look rumpled. Ready?"

I nodded and allowed Finn to lift me into his arms, tucking me close against his chest before he shot into the sky.

"I know I've thanked you before, but I'm so glad you didn't give up on me." He swooped over the houses and away from town.

"I'd never do such a thing. I know you'd given up, but we just needed the missing puzzle piece. It wasn't until I had the idea about dragon flame that it came together."

"And your visit to Wild Wing."

"Yes, that was an unforgettable experience."

"Torrin and Madeline stayed at mine last night," Finn said. "He couldn't stop talking about how you got him free. Madeline really wants to meet you, so she can thank you."

"I'm certain I'll meet them soon." I stifled a smile. I'd done a little late-night negotiating with Cythera and Maverick to ensure there'd be a happy ending for Torrin and Madeline.

Finn laughed and spun in the air.

I hissed at him. "Don't do that! And tell me where we're going. This doesn't feel like a short flight."

"We're here!" He dropped closer to the ground. "I thought you'd want to say goodbye to the hatchling." Finn landed carefully and set me down.

I looked around. "She's leaving Crimson Cove?"

A flicker of sadness entered Finn's eyes. "I've got no choice but to let her go. Once the dragons knew she was here, the game was up."

"No names were mentioned when we met Willow."

"I know, and I appreciate that. Dragons are smart, and they'd already figured things out. And Rembrandt, or rather, René, blabbed everything in an attempt to win back their favor."

"I'm glad his efforts failed."

"Once I got free, I found Willow waiting for me at the animal sanctuary. We had a long conversation, and then I introduced her to the hatchling. Honestly, it just about broke my heart, but she was so happy to meet another dragon that I knew I had to let her go. I don't want to, though. I'm so ridiculously in love with her, but it's wrong to keep her."

The ground shuddered beneath our feet, and Willow came into view. "I appreciate how hard this is for you, Finn, but I'm glad you're doing the right thing. And so is the hatchling."

The hatchling shot out from behind Willow and charged toward us. She threw herself at Finn, knocking him off his feet, and wrapped her tail around me so I went with them. We rolled together in a jumble of feathers, fur, and scales, the hatchling making noises of delight in the back of her throat.

Willow looked on, happiness radiating from her. "She wouldn't be this joyful if you hadn't taken the best care of her. I see how much she loves you."

Finn struggled out from under the rambunctious baby and wrapped a strong arm around her wings to keep her under control. "She's a part of my family. I never had a real family growing up, but when we met, it felt so right."

"And because of that, and because you looked after her so well and cared for her after she was cruelly abandoned, I've convinced the other dragons that there'll be no repercussions against you. You did wrong, but you did it for the right reasons. And it wouldn't be fair to split you two up permanently."

I stared up at Willow. "Finn can keep her?"

"No, but whenever you wish to see the hatchling, you may visit her in Wild Wing."

Finn grinned and wiped his face with the back of his hand to remove tears. "I'd love that."

"The invitation extends to you as well, Juno. The infant has been most vocal in her demands about continuing her friendship with you."

"I can think of nothing I'd like more," I said.

"There is one more thing," Willow said. "I understand you have yet to decide on her name."

"Oh! I didn't name her because I'd only grow more attached," Finn said.

"She cannot be called 'baby' or 'hatchling' forever," Willow said. "Give me your suggestions. You must have thought of some names."

"Silver. Sparkle. Cinder. Bianca. Asha. Luna. Lucy. Pearl." Finn drew in a breath and smiled. "I guess I've been thinking about her name more than I realized."

"They're all beautiful," I said. "I like Cinder. She's certainly free with her flame."

Willow nodded. "Cinder. I approve. From now on, she'll be known by that name. Now, we must go. I need to introduce this baby to her extended family. And I believe you have a wedding to attend."

Finn checked the time. "We should get going."

"Just one more moment, Juno. Walk with me while Finn says his goodbyes." Willow turned and strode away.

"I won't be long." I hurried after Willow.

Willow reached behind a boulder and pulled out a smooth red stone. "I believe this is yours." She set it on the ground in front of me.

I approached the stone, and the second I drew near, a familiar rush of ancient power rolled toward me. I drew in a breath. It was my missing power.

"I recognized your energy," Willow said. "When we fought in Wild Wing and I grabbed you, I sensed how old your magic was, and I recalled collecting a stone to add to my hoard that had the same magical signature. Am I right in thinking that once belonged to you?"

I couldn't speak, so shocked to have my power back. I nodded.

"Then it is yours. Power should never be taken from its rightful owner, just as an infant dragon should never be taken from its family. Now, both our dreams can come true. We have everything we need."

I choked out a thank you, unable to tear my gaze from the stone.

Willow hesitated. "This gift has given you much to think about. I trust I've done the right thing?"

"Yes," I stuttered out. "I'd almost given up on finding it. I'd grown content with what I have."

"Dragon blessings on you, Juno. I'm certain you'll do the right thing."

The hatchling dodged over, squeaked a goodbye at me, then took to the wing with Willow, and they soared above the tree line and vanished.

"Hey, Juno. We need to move," Finn called out.

"I'll be right with you." This was no ordinary stone I'd been given. I had a feeling deep in my gut that, when I united this stone with the other pieces, I'd have everything I needed.

Finn appeared. He joined me and looked at the stone. "What you got there?"

"A big decision to make," I said.

"Unless you want us to be late, you'll need to make that decision after the wedding."

I sucked in a shaky breath. "Could you look after it for me?"

"Sure." He lifted the stone and put it inside his jacket pocket. "Now, let's go see two angels get married, shall we?"

⁂

Amidst the shimmering celestial splendor, the grand event of the century unfolded - the long-awaited wedding of Cythera and Maverick was here. Two angels who'd defied murder, a poisoning attempt, and a spiky-tongued mother-in-law were getting their wish to marry.

The venue was divine, located in an angel-exclusive dimension of mists and warm sun that had been opened just for today for all guests.

I sat on Zandra's lap since it was a crush for seats. Half the town was here, along with a host of angels, regular and higher, their wings fluttering with excitement.

The ceremony room was resplendent in its ethereal white radiance and glistened under the illumination of countless orbs as if the heavens had also gathered to witness the union. Maybe they had. This wedding was one of a kind.

"Maverick looks nervous," Vorana whispered to us, comfy in her seat, with Sage on her lap.

"He's got to be. He's about to spend the rest of his very long life with Cythera," Zandra murmured.

"He looks happy," I said. "And so he should. When Cythera relaxes, she's a delight."

"When have you ever seen her relax?" Sage asked.

"There was that one occasion when... no, not then. How about... not that occasion, either. Hmmm... maybe we'll see her relax today."

Zandra chuckled. "Some people thrive on stress. She's one of them."

"Maverick isn't. They're an excellent balance for each other," I said.

The air was alive with the hum of angelic music and soft whispers of anticipation that fluttered like delicate feathers. I took a moment to search for Amelia, Maverick's mother. She looked remarkably calm, and there wasn't a hint of shrewish disapproval. I was glad she'd finally left the couple alone and stopped meddling in their happiness.

The main wedding pavilion, where the ceremony would take place, stood like a beacon of heavenly elegance in front of the guests. Its walls were adorned with intricate patterns of celestial symbols, each glowing with a faint luminescence.

The higher angels, resplendent in their glowing robes, formed an honor guard around the pavilion to welcome the start of the ceremony. Tinkerbell was there, proudly sitting on Bilious's shoulder. She spotted me and lifted a paw.

The music shifted, and the mutterings stilled. Cythera appeared at the end of the aisle, and for a moment, I had no breath in my lungs. Her gown was a masterpiece of magical couture, shimmering in hues of moonlit silver and opalescent blue, its fabric seemingly woven from stardust and moonbeams. Intricate patterns of constellations adorned the bodice, and delicate trails of twinkling lights traced down the skirt, imbuing her with otherworldly elegance.

"Whoa! That's fancy," Zandra whispered. "I figured she'd go for a white pantsuit. Something sensible."

"These angels do nothing by halves when it's an occasion like this," Sorcha said. "She looks incredible."

As Cythera moved, the dress radiated a soft glow that matched the rhythm of her slow footsteps. Tiny sparks of light danced along the edges of her gown, leaving traces of stardust as she walked. And she wasn't walking alone. Finn was giving her away!

"When did that happen?" I asked Zandra.

She shrugged. "No clue. Maybe it's Cythera's way of letting him know she's glad he didn't get charged with murder."

"I knew she was fond of him," I said. "Finn must be thrilled."

Finn's grin was wide and his joy obvious as he walked proudly, nodding at people and letting Cythera take her time to experience her final walk as a single angel.

Cythera's wings fluttered gracefully as she passed us. Her golden hair cascaded like a waterfall of sunlight, adorned with delicate star-shaped pins. And as her gaze met mine, she nodded.

Such a simple gesture, but I appreciated it. Despite her sternest efforts to avoid it, we were friends, and I was delighted she was about to get her happily ever after with Maverick.

I turned my attention to the front of the aisle. Maverick stood there, a stunned expression on his face. "Uh-oh. He looks like he's about to faint. Take a breath. You've got this."

"He can't believe how well Cythera scrubs up," Zandra said.

Maverick's expression quickly transformed into an elated smile as he took in every detail of Cythera's gown.

"Aww. He's in love." Sorcha squeezed Denver's hand, who was settled beside her and happily taking the best care of my friend.

"Maverick has always cared more than he let on," I said. "He just didn't want to scare Cythera away by being too soppy around her."

"They were picked to be together because they're soulmates." Vorana dabbed her eyes with a tissue.

"Don't start crying already!" Sage rested her paws on Vorana's chest and licked away the tears.

As Cythera approached Maverick, their eyes locked, and it seemed as if the rest of the world vanished as they stared at each other. The cascade of flowers in Cythera's hand trembled.

Maverick let out a laugh of pure joy, and everyone sighed. He reached out and took her hand in his. "You're more breathtaking than I could have ever imagined."

She looked down at her gown and blushed. "It's not terrible."

"It's perfect. So are you." Maverick turned to the higher angel celebrant. "Please, marry us."

The guests laughed.

As Cythera and Maverick stood beneath a radiant archway, their hands entwined, their eyes locked in a gaze that spoke volumes of the journey they'd taken to get there, a hushed reverence settled over the gathered angels, friends, and family.

"Before we begin, we're sharing our day with another couple." Cythera gestured for someone to join them.

Torrin Conner, dressed in a smart, dark suit, and a stunning redhead with a flash of radiant green scales running up the side of her neck and onto her freckled cheeks, appeared, their hands clasped. They dashed along the aisle and stood beside Cythera and Maverick.

"Many of you know Torrin," Cythera said. "He's found his true love, and he wanted to waste no time in uniting with her."

"Since we've been given so much for our special day, we wanted to share it with them," Maverick said. "We can't let another happy couple go without. Welcome, friends."

"And the faster they marry, the harder it'll be for their families to split them up." I sat alert on Zandra's lap, happy to see my plan had come together.

"Did you know about this surprise addition?" Zandra asked.

"I put in a word on their behalf and explained how we found Torrin in a difficult situation. The dragons approve. They gave the union their blessing," I said. "And by having Torrin and Madeline here, it's a warning to the dragon shifters not to mess with them. They have the support of the dragons, the angels, and us."

"You're always meddling, Juno," Sage grumbled.

"And look what my marvelous meddling has created."

Sage grunted but gently head-butted me.

Maverick and Torrin shook hands, and the brides exchanged greetings.

"Now we're all here, let us begin," the celebrant said.

An angel wedding is long and complicated, and during the hours of chanting, singing, and exchanging of various items, I napped on Zandra's lap, but nothing of note was missed.

I roused when the celebrant announced the final vows were to be said. Torrin and Madeline had already wed and stood to the side to watch the final portion of the ceremony.

Maverick's voice broke the silence. "Cythera, your grace, your strength, and your unwavering dedication to a cause you're passionate about has taught me the true meaning of life. I promise to cherish you, to uplift you, and to stand by your side through every celestial dance and every shadowed night."

Cythera's eyes tightened. She extracted a piece of paper from a hidden pocket in her gown. "Maverick, you are acceptably symmetrical."

"Is that it?" Zandra muttered.

Cythera cleared her throat. "Our union is welcomed by our families. We will not be a disappointment."

"Oh, dear." Vorana hid her face in her hands. "She's gone into Robot Cythera mode."

"Come on, Cythera," I whispered. "Crack that veneer and show Maverick you care."

A murmur of unease crackled through the guests. Amelia had stiffened in her seat and was glaring daggers at Cythera for being so wooden with her precious son.

Finn inched forward and whispered into Cythera's ear, and my cat hearing picked it up. "Remember how we practiced. Just say it. No one will laugh."

I held my breath.

Cythera shifted from foot to foot. "Maverick, I like you. I think highly of you. You... you make me happy. We will be happier together." She shot forward and kissed his cheek.

A soft murmur of approval rippled through the gathering.

"That's big," Vorana said. "That's basically Cythera announcing she's head over heels in love with the guy."

"And Maverick knows it." I relaxed against Zandra's belly as Maverick's dazzling smile almost blinded me.

After a few words from the celebrant, Maverick slipped a ring onto Cythera's finger. "With this ring, I bind my heart to yours, my love to yours, and my soul to yours. I am yours in every world, in every lifetime, and through every eternity."

Cythera's cheeks were pink as she slid the ring onto Maverick's finger and repeated the words.

A tender smile graced Maverick's lips as their eyes met, a silent communion that spoke of their happiness. With a breathless pause, they leaned forward, their lips meeting in a kiss.

The assembled angels bashed their wings together, while others whooped and blasted harmless spells and sparkles into the air. Maverick and Cythera drew back, their eyes shining, their fingers still intertwined.

"I never thought I'd see it happen, but it looks like miracles are real." Sorcha grinned as she wiped away a stray tear.

"Now it's time to party!" Zandra plucked at her dress. "I should have worn something with an expandable waistline because I intend to eat one of everything at the buffet."

Hand in hand, Cythera and Maverick began their walk along the aisle, their steps light and buoyant, their wings fluttering. As they passed, guests offered their heartfelt congratulations, their smiles warm and genuine as star-shaped confetti was tossed with abandon.

Torrin and Madeline were right behind them, happily accepting congratulations, too. Torrin caught my eye and winked, mouthing a thank you.

Maverick's gaze also met mine, and he offered me a relieved smile, a silent acknowledgment of the journey we'd all been on to bring them to this moment.

I purred softly, a contented sound that resonated my satisfaction at being a part of this celebration to unite two perfect couples.

The guests slowly filed outside. The grounds were breathtaking, with pristine white arches and lush, blooming flowers. Angels of all ages mingled, their wings unfurled and their white gowns and suits dazzling.

As the cameras clicked and flashes illuminated the scene, the guests struck poses and exchanged playful banter. Even some of the more reserved guests couldn't help but break into smiles, caught up in the joyous atmosphere. I even saw Remus holding a sun parasol as he jigged with a striking-looking female werewolf.

Near to the staged area for photos, a long table was laden with a delectable array of food and drinks. There were trays of delicate finger sandwiches, fresh fruits arranged like works of art, and crystal goblets that held a sparkling concoction that shimmered with the light.

A table centerpiece held a magnificent cake, a Crimson Cove original masterpiece crafted from layers of fluffy angel food cake, with each tier decorated in intricate patterns of swirls and delicate flowers. Binky guarded the cake, and Tia stood nearby, looking nervous.

I pointed them out to Zandra, and we walked over.

Binky's ears pricked as we arrived. "Hey! Enjoy the wedding?"

"I slept for most of it, but I enjoyed the end," I said. "Tia, your cake is magnificent. Worthy to be presented at any angel wedding."

Tia smiled. "This is the first cake. I've baked five in total. They're all coming out at various points during the day. I'm exhausted. Happy I made them what they wanted, but my blender is on its knees!"

Zandra drooled over the food. "I knew I should have gone for stretchy waist pants, but Vorana insisted on this dumb dress."

"You look great. And Cythera looks stunning." Tia turned when someone called her name. "Binky, guard the cake. I won't be long."

Binky stood, her fur fluffed, and her gaze narrowed.

My gaze drifted to where Cythera and Maverick were sharing a laugh and hugs with their guests, and contentment settled over me, mingling with a hint of nostalgia. This reminded me of my own wedding, surrounded by goddesses, gods, higher beings, and friends. That had been many lifetimes ago. A lifetime I'd just about given up on ever returning to.

Finn and Torrin approached, accompanied by his striking new bride, Madeline. Her genuine smile warmed my heart as she extended her hand toward me.

"Juno, I can't thank you enough for helping make this day happen," she said. "Finn told us what you did in Wild Wing and how you persuaded Cythera and Maverick to share all of this with us."

I rested a paw in her hand. "It was my pleasure. Everyone deserves a happy ending." I introduced Madeline to Zandra, who was distracted by all the treats but managed a friendly greeting.

As Zandra moved along the table, a plate in hand, Finn gestured his head to the side, and I excused myself and followed him a short distance until we were alone.

"I've been curious about something," he said.

I twitched my whiskers. "How you'll spend your days living as a free angel now you don't have a dragon hunting you or an infant to care for?"

He grinned. "I have thoughts on that."

"Do tell."

Finn chuckled. "Cythera's given me a few weeks off. I'm going to check into my dad's story. I'm not so sure he was being honest with me."

I hesitated. Should I reveal what Torrin told me? "You may not like what you find."

"Sure, but I need to know. We all need to know where we came from. Go back to our roots from time to time."

I considered that, and I couldn't disagree. This was Finn's quest, not mine. "Safe travels. We'll be here when you return. And in Cythera's absence, while she honeymoons with Maverick, I may make some tweaks to Angel Force."

Finn laughed. "Don't touch the place, or she'll skin you."

I glanced at the happy couple. "She's mellowing, so I should survive."

He was quiet for a moment. "That red stone Willow gifted you. What's the story behind it?"

I tensed. I'd taken the stone from Finn and hidden it in the basement apartment, but it had never been far from my thoughts. "It's... complicated."

Finn leaned closer, his gaze curious. "I figured as much. Complicated how?"

"It's a piece of my past," I admitted. "A piece that has the potential to shape my future. Or rather, return it to how it used to be. Go back to my roots, if you like."

His brow furrowed. "This has to do with your weird magic?"

I sighed, my gaze wandering back to the newlyweds. "I've always been content living with my wonderful witch, being her familiar. But I've also had a long-held dream. But now, I'm unsure if..."

"If it's still the dream you want to catch?" Finn's expression softened.

"It would mean big change."

"Change can be exciting and unsettling."

I nodded, my heart heavy with uncertainty. "Exactly. I love Zandra, and I've always envisioned our future together. But this stone represents a world I once knew, a world of power and destiny. I can't help but wonder what it means for me now I have it back."

"Change doesn't mean letting go of the past." Finn's voice was gentle. "It's about embracing new opportunities while carrying the lessons you've learned."

"You sound worryingly wise."

"There's this cat I've been hanging out with. She's a bit snooty, but she knows her stuff. I've learned things from her." He crouched beside me. "And I'm here to support you, no matter what path you choose. Zandra will support you, too. We all will."

As I looked at my friends enjoying the party, my wonderful witch with cake around her mouth as she joined Randal, I sighed again. The uncertainty about my future remained, but so did the unwavering bond I shared with all these people.

Finn nudged me. "I heard a rumor Maverick ordered a special salmon cake for a certain fluffy feline and her friends. Want to see if it's true?"

"I'll race you to it!" I leaned against him, a smile on my face, ready to face whatever the future had in store for me.

About the Author

K.E. O'Connor (Karen) is a mystery author living in the beautiful British countryside. She loves all things mystery, animals, and cake. If you want to practice spells, solve a few murders, and spend time with amazing witches and their talking familiars, join her weekly newsletter.

Sign up today:

Newsletter: https://BookHip.com/GXDVFRA
Website: www.keoconnor.com
Facebook: www.facebook.com/keoconnorauthor

Also By

Witch Haven: Welcome to Witch Haven, where nothing is what it seems. Meet four fabulous witches as they struggle with their destinies, deal with misfiring magic, murder, and the Magic Council.

Crypt Witches: Meet Tempest Crypt, a witch who swallows demons, and Wiggles, her mini talking hellhound, while you enjoy magical murder and intrigue.

Lorna Shadow: A cozy mystery series set in the fun world of a personal assistant who sees ghosts. Meet Lorna, her ditzy sidekick, Helen, and Flipper, the dog who senses ghosts, as they solve crimes and save the day.

Holly Holmes: An adorable cozy culinary mystery series set in the beautiful village of Audley St. Mary. Each book is full of treats, murder, and twists. Join Holly and Meatball, her clue-hunting dog, as they solve murders and eat cake.

www.ingramcontent.com/pod-product-compliance
Lightning Source LLC
Chambersburg PA
CBHW061538210726
48287CB00006B/2004